PUPPET SKIN

(OR: MAY YOU GROW UP
TO BE A BEAUTIFUL LOG)

Danger Slater

FUNGASM PRESS

FUNGASM PRESS
PO BOX 10065
PORTLAND, OR 97296

AN ERASERHEAD PRESS COMPANY
www.ERASERHEADPRESS.com

WWW.ERASERHEADPRESS.COM

ISBN: 978-1-62105-223-4

Here is a list of people who, in some capacity, helped bring this book to life:

Lisa LeStrange, John Skipp, Rose O'Keefe, Katie McCann, Lori Hettler, Jessica McHugh, Kevin Strange, Carlton Mellick III, Jeff Burk, and all my friends and family in Bizarro and beyond.

Thank you.

To my mom.

We made it.

"One must still have chaos within oneself to give birth to a dancing star."

—Friedrich Nietzsche, *Thus Spoke Zarathrustra*

One

Hannah lived in a big house in the suburbs and she did her homework every night and she ate all of her acorn mash because she was always told that acorn mash would make her strong, and she emptied the dishwasher when it was full and she took out the trash when it started to smell and she always remembered to floss after brushing and both of her parents were puppets.

All adults were puppets.

Hannah was not a puppet herself. She was made of meat. Her body was full of muscles and bones. She had brown hair like a coconut and brown eyes that seemed to glow orange when the sun hit them in just the right way. Her skin was not a thin layer of acrylic paint slathered on top of hard cedar flesh. Her skin was warm and soft to the touch, and although blood flowed through her veins the same way tree sap flowed through pinewood, she knew she wasn't a puppet because she had a heart that beat in her chest like every breath she exhaled was a rock n' roll concert.

Hannah was very much alive.

That wasn't to say that adults weren't alive. Because they were. They were just alive *differently*.

As children, her parents were biological too. Just like Hannah. Everyone started out biological. That's how it worked.

When Hannah threw tantrums or acted emotional or irrational, her parents said they understood what she was going through, though that never stopped them from reacting to her pain with the calculated precision of a mousetrap. They'd respond quickly and in always the same way. They said that a big part of growing up meant letting go of all the fragile branches that caused her grief.

She had been shown a few grainy photographs of her parents as babies. Helpless balls of discolored flesh. Weak. Useless. Just one bad day, one small mistake away from complete and irreversible oblivion. Death was there in those pictures too. Watching. Waiting. And yet, despite that, her parents looked happy back then. Their bodies were still pliable. They smiled.

When she looked at her mom and dad now, when she looked at their wooden movements and glassy doll eyes, Hannah found it hard to believe that they once possessed a heart like her own. That they used to travel through life completely untethered, unstrung, unencumbered, and the only thing that controlled them then were the whims and expectations of their own puppet parents.

Her mother always told her that after she became a puppet too, she'd finally understand what a gift being young is.

Two

The silence that hung from the chandelier felt as heavy as the shadows that engulfed everything that lay outside of its splayed, saffron light. Crimson drapes and purple upholstery sucked up what was left of the daytime like a tissue in a puddle of oil. The only illumination in the dining room came from a single light overhead, shining down like an interrogation lamp.

It was under this lamp that Hannah sat.

Her mother and father sat at the table too. Just beyond the light's grasp. In the darkness, in repose. Limbs limp. Heads down. Completely motionless. Piles of lumber. Puppets didn't breathe. They didn't jingle-jangle like pocket change. Puppets only moved when they needed to.

"It's almost Friday," her mother then said, her voice like a chainsaw ripping through the forest as her strings went taut and her body suddenly sprung to life. "I remember the day I graduated middle school. It was the day I truly felt my life began. Before then I was a zygote. A tadpole. I was unformed. Unfinished. Childhood was such a useless blur; I don't even remember it. It was like an ugly dream. The day I graduated middle school was the day I finally became a person."

She leaned in towards Hannah so that her face was shaded in sharp, toothlike patterns. "So many wonderful things are waiting for you on the other side of that ceremony, Hannah. Once they attach your strings, everything will be different. Better. You will no longer be a child. You will be a puppet. You will be all grown up."

"I guess," Hannah mumbled without looking up. She

languidly forked at her acorn mash as a tendril of chocolate hair fell across her forehead. She didn't bother pushing it away.

"I'm sorry," her mother said. "I couldn't hear you. What did you just say?"

"I said I guess."

"You *guess*?" her mother went.

"Yeah, I guess," Hannah repeated herself. "I don't know what you want me to do, Mom. Jump for joy? Sing a song? Throw myself a parade? Graduation is Friday. I am well aware of that."

Her mother shook her head and let out an exasperated sigh. "Are we really going to keep doing this, Hannah? Aren't you tired of having this same old conversation, over and over again? And this close to graduation too?"

Hannah didn't respond. Her mother continued:

"Look, I don't think I'm saying anything to you that you don't already know. You're about to become a young woman, dear. And a young woman doesn't need to act like a spoiled little baby every time she doesn't want to do something. Especially when it's something as important as this. You can't keep goofing off forever. Life is not a joke, or a game. It's not an appointment at the doctor's office that you can cry your way out of. You HAVE to get serious about the future, because time is up and, for you, the future is already here."

"I am serious," Hannah protested, laying her utensil down. "Why do you always hafta say that? I'm just sitting here. I'm not even doing anything wrong."

"C'mon," her mother rolled her plastic eyes. "You're not fooling anyone. You've barely touched your food."

"I'm not hungry right now."

"That is exactly what I'm talking about, Hannah," her mompet said. "A young woman would be hungry when she was supposed to be hungry, and she wouldn't question it or complain. That's what being responsible is. I mean, look at you. How serious could you possibly be? You're not even a puppet yet. Not even a little bit..."

Her mom pinched her.

"Ow!" yelped Hannah.

"See?" her mother said. "You're all squishy. Like a jellyfish. How do you expect to survive in this world when your body is soft like a jellyfish?"

From the black void in the ceiling, her parent's strings came. Thick strings, seemingly from outer space itself. They affixed themselves up and down her mom's arms and legs. Driven like Holy Nails through the palms of her hands. Screwed into her feet like tent pegs. Even out of the top of her skull the strings came. They compelled her to move. To tilt her head in that judgmental manner in which it was always tilted. To move her nutcracker-like jaw up and down and speak the words that ceaselessly came out of her mouth:

"What do you want to be when you grow up?"

This was a question that Hannah had been asked a thousand times before. Offered to her first as an infant. Echoed again and again through toddlerhood and adolescence. The sentiment rang hollow back then. Not a real question, just a thing people said when they had to say something. A congeniality. A way to fill up the empty air. To assess, to evaluate, to connect with a grubby little human.

But now, on the verge of Hannah becoming a puppet herself, the same question she'd been asked time and again throughout her life no longer felt like an abstraction. It was heavy. And graceless. And gigantic. And real. And it needled at her every time she heard it with increasingly desperate and hungry claws.

"I don't know," Hannah huffed back in response.

This was the answer by which she always replied.

It was the answer by which she replied again.

Through the strings plugged into the back of her parents' skulls the puppetfeed flowed. It dribbled like oatmeal into the empty cavities in their heads. A thick white pabulum the same consistency of Hannah's own acorn mash, although she knew the recipe in that tube was very different than what she ate. There were other ingredients in there, ingredients that were especially blended to nurture a puppet's anatomy: vitamins and chemicals and supplements and lacquer. It was fed to her parents intravenously, passed through the main string on top. Adults had no need to eat. Not the way Hannah did. Not the way animals did. They had no need to chew. Masticate and digest. Still, the family gathered at the dinner table every night just as the family had gathered ever since Hannah was little. It was ritual. Her dad in his chair, her mom in hers. Empty plates before both of them, forever untouched.

Her mother shook her head. "It's always 'I don't know' with you, isn't it Hannah? That's not an acceptable answer anymore, dear. You know your cousin Bette is getting ready to attach her strings too? And she's 2 years younger than you. What does that tell you about yourself?"

"Yeah? Well, hooray for her," Hannah sarcastically said. "Isn't Bette just wonderful?"

"That's right," her mompet said. "You're trying to be flippant with me, but Bette *is* wonderful. SHE'S thinking about the next step. SHE'S thinking about the future. SHE is going to be very successful one day. I hate to break it to you, Hannah, but whether you like it or not, there's going to be a tomorrow. Life is going to continue to exist after the 8th grade."

Hannah squinted her eyes and stabbed her dinner with her fork. Even this argument felt cursory. Rote. Routine, right down to the part where Hannah's mother turned to her father and said, "Aren't I right, dear?" And her father, who had been laying there like a pile of driftwood the whole time would amble awake and say, "Listen to your mother," before returning back to the flaccid position from which he rose.

After that, silence and shadow once again enveloped the room like a wool blanket had been pulled over the conversation. This was how dinner concluded every day. Hannah would begrudgingly finish eating her acorn mash and then she'd empty the dishwasher and then she'd take out the trash and then she'd brush her teeth and climb into her bed and then she'd go to sleep. Every day this played out the exact same way. Every day, that is, except for one.

This one.

"I want to dance," Hannah suddenly blurted out.

Her mom, who had resumed her dead-eyed stare at the wall, snapped back into consciousness.

"Wh-what was that?" she said.

"You asked me what I wanted to do when I grow up?" Hannah said. "Well, I'm answering you. I want to dance."

"What do you mean dance?" her mompet said. "Like, *dance* dance? Like, professionally?"

"Yeah," said Hannah. "Or maybe not professionally. I don't know. I don't think about it like that. Thing is, it doesn't really matter much to me how it happens. I just like to dance. It makes me feel happy. You asked me. I answered. That's what I want to do with my life. I want to dance."

"Darling," her mother cooed as she raised a stiff hand and laid it on the top of her child's head. "That is the stupidest thing I've ever heard. Do you have any idea how difficult dancing is? Few puppets possess that innate ability. Fewer still have the temperament to hone it into anything worthwhile. And even fewer than that are able to support themselves and lead productive and fulfilling lives with that sort of narrow and, ultimately, fruitless skill set. And not for nothing, but I've seen you walk. You're not exactly the paradigm of grace. What are you going to do when your strings get all tangled up to the point where you're unable to move? You'll end up a crumpled lump on the floor. You'll be of no use to anybody."

"But I'm not a puppet!" Hannah cried out. "I don't have strings to get tangled. I can still do what I want."

"Bah," her mompet brushed off her daughter's concerns. "You don't know WHAT you want yet."

Three

Hannah spent the rest of the night locked in her room reading about infectious diseases on the internet. Influenza and meningitis and tuberculous and typhoid. Then onto rarer stuff like smallpox and bubonic plague and Gerstmann-Sträussler-Scheinker Syndrome.

She looked at her body in the mirror. Her complexion was as wan as the waxing moon and her skinny knees looked like garlic knots stuck to her legs. She was gangly. Awkward. An amalgam of disproportioned parts hastily assembled into something vaguely recognizable as human. She wondered if she was the only one to look at her body as if it were this alien thing. An uncomfortable suit two sizes too small. Her arms and legs felt like anchors, leftovers from some antediluvian era when people had some sort of need for such long and gawky limbs. Puppet parts are all perfectly symmetrical. They are crafted with forethought, fidelity, and care. Human beings are a mess. She grabbed a roll of fat from her belly and squeezed it between her fingers. She squeezed it as hard as she could, until it turned purple. She was trapped inside this sausage casing she called her skin.

The internet also told her that inside her body were bacteria. Trillions of bacteria, filling her up like the sands on a beach. They lived in symbiosis with her. They were necessary for her survival. They were her silent partners. They were part Hannah, too.

But, she read on, not all the bacteria inside of you were benign. Sometimes they arrive with malicious intent. Sometimes the bacteria will try to kill you. Sometimes a virus will enter your body and pillage it until there is nothing

17

left. Sometimes a parasite gets in and demands more than its fair share. And more than that, death doesn't always have to slowly invade like a foreign army, riding in on a sneeze or an unwashed railing. Sometimes your own body just messes up, all on its own. Your heart skips a beat and it seizes up, or your blood flows the wrong way and short circuits your brain.

It will happen. One day, it will.

Inside of her, things flourished. Things were born and they died. Lives were lived. She was the terrarium for an invisible universe.

Being made of meat is a terrifying amount of responsibility.

She looked up. Even in her bedroom, the ceiling was an empty black void, just like it was in the dining room. Just like it was in every ceiling in her house and every other house that was ever built.

All ceilings are voids.

In fact, the whole sky was full of empty voids like this. The cerulean calm of a summer's day was always interrupted by these Swiss cheese holes. They rested like dark dinner plates on the sky's blue tablecloth. It's where the strings came from. They came out of the holes like the wires running down a cell phone tower.

They say there is a Puppeteer up there. That there is someone in the sky who controls everything that happens here on the ground. That he was the one pulling the strings. But no one could confirm his existence. You were just supposed to trust that he was up there. Believe in him. Have faith. Hannah wasn't totally convinced that such a person could even exist. Or *should* exist. Hannah didn't want a man in the sky to tell her on the ground where she should be moving.

The void in her bedroom was a constant reminder that, soon, she too was expected to attach her strings. To turn to timber like the rest of the world.

Her parents didn't have to worry about viruses and diseases. They were not going to suddenly come down with the bubonic plague or Gerstmann-Sträussler-Scheinker Syndrome. They didn't have blood to turn poison or brains to get cloudy. They were free from that kind of uncertainty.

Of course, wood too can rot if left untreated.

But then again, without proper care, everything will rot eventually.

Four

Gray smoke filled her chest. She could feel her lungs constricting. Like a hug from the inside. It was warm and dangerous and made her feel both afraid and alive. When she exhaled, the cloud hung for a moment in the air in front of her, as if it were waving goodbye. The wind blew. Hugs are ephemeral. A cigarette can only love you for a few fleeting moments.

"What are you assholes lookin' at?" Jordan spat at a group of kids innocently walking by. They all averted their eyes to the sidewalk. Jordan flared her nostrils and let smoke pour out of them as if she were a dragon. "Assholes need to mind their own damn business," she mumbled to Hannah as the kids scuttled into the school.

"Yeah, they were totally being assholes," Hannah insincerely parroted her friend.

Jordan smirked.

Both girls took a simultaneous drag from their respective cigarettes and tried not to cough.

Theirs was a tiny rebellion. Blue language and blind angst and a pack of Marlboro Reds purloined from the corner grocery store. Small rainbows they cast upon a dull and endless pond.

"You're only hurting yourself."

That's what a teacher would say if they caught them smoking. It was a logical appeal and, intrinsically, Hannah knew this statement to be true. But this cigarette was also liberating, in a way. Hurting yourself was the ultimate act of control. In those short moments when the poison air filled her wholly, and she held it in for as long as she could, she was able to conquer helplessness. To overcome it. To laugh at it.

"Man, I can't wait to get out of this crap town," said Jordan. "This place is like a lead ball strapped to my ankle. Everyone around me is so stupid all the time." She looked at Hannah. "Except you, of course."

"Can I have another cigarette?" Hannah asked.

Jordan pulled a crooked butt from the crumpled box and handed it to her friend. Hannah lit it and inhaled. She felt sick to her stomach.

"Once we get out of this dumb school, we're not gonna have to deal with being told what to do anymore," Jordan said. "Imagine it. We'll finally be free of all this nonsense. Waking up and doing homework and eating that disgusting acorn slop they feed us every day. We'll finally be free to do whatever we want."

"But what about when they attach your strings?" Hannah asked. "Someone's gotta be pulling those strings, right?"

"Are you kidding me? I'm not gonna let them attach no strings to me," Jordan scoffed.

"Everyone gets strings when they become adults," said Hannah. "That's how it works."

"I don't care how it works," the girl defiantly replied. "We're better than that, Hannah. I don't need no puppeteer to tell me what to do. I mean, could you even imagine this same kinda bullshit continuing on forever and ever? No way! I'm getting outta here first chance I get and I ain't lookin' back."

"But where would you go?" asked Hannah.

"Huh?" went Jordan.

"Well, if you could go anywhere in the world, where would that be?"

"Hmm," said Jordan. "I guess I hadn't considered all that. I supposed I'd go to The City. Have you ever been to The City?"

"No," Hannah replied.

"I've been there before," said Jordan.

"You have?"

"Well, no. I haven't. But we used to drive really close to it when I was little. My mom was dating some guy who lived right near the gully. Trevor or Gregor or Travis or Babbit or Rabbit or Janet or Mamet or Granite or Marble or Stonewell or Stonewall or Jack or Sonny or Benny or something like that. I don't remember his name. He was an asshole too. Just like everyone else."

"What was it like?" Hannah asked.

"My mom's boyfriend?"

"No, The City. What was it like?"

"It almost looked fake," said Jordan. "The skyline was like the backdrop in a movie, or painted on the wall behind a late-night talk show host. So perfect against the sky, it's hard to believe it's even a real place. It looked like it was drawn in pen on the horizon."

"I'd love to see it for myself someday," said Hannah.

"If I could, I'd leave this crap town tomorrow and go to The City and pursue modeling. Fashion modeling. That's what I've always wanted to do. Do you think I could be a fashion model, Hannah?"

"Oh my god, Jordan, you absolutely could. You're so pretty," she replied. And Hannah wasn't lying to her friend when she said that. She wasn't placating Jordan to protect her ego or simply being agreeable because it was easier than being contrary. Jordan *was* pretty. She had a natural beauty that, even if unspoken, was self-evident. But more than that, she also knew how to augment her looks to her favor, too. She adorned herself with bracelets and jewelry and had big swooping chains hanging around her neck that clanged together like church bells if she moved her head too fast. Her eyelids were shadowed black, coming to wingtips on either side of her face. This was accented by cherry lipstick and rosy luminizer and held together by these thin piqued eyebrows that arched like gothic buttresses across her grimaced forehead.

She tried teaching Hannah about makeup. Hannah would practice putting on eyeliner and lipstick and blush. But it never looked quite right to her. It seemed strange. Uncomfortable. Fake, even. To her, the more layers of makeup she put on, the closer it looked to the same kind of paint that coated the faces of her own puppet parents.

"You know how much money a model can make?" said Jordan.

"No," said Hannah.

"Lots of money," Jordan replied.

"How much is a lot?"

"I don't know. A million dollars? Ten million? Enough money to be happy," Jordan answered. "I'm going to have the best life ever."

"Yeah," Hannah exhaled a plume of smoke, once again agreeing with her friend. "Me, too."

Five

"Hannah, are you paying attention?" Mr. Mahogany said.

Hannah looked up at her teacher. His black eyes glistened as he looked back at her.

"Of course, Mr. Mahogany," she replied.

"This is important, dear," said the teacher, motioning to the illustration on the chalkboard. The thin outline of a child was bent over at the waist with the needle-pointed ends of puppet strings just inches from his curved spine. They reached towards him like squid tentacles ready to seize. "You need to make sure that when they attach your strings, they get attached correctly. The placement is vital. One wrong move and you can screw up your entire transformation. And if you screw up your transformation, you screw up your whole future."

"I know, Mr. Mahogany," she said to the puppet man. "I am rapt. I am interested."

But she wasn't interested. Not at all. She was still thinking about what Jordan had said earlier. About The City. Hannah had been enamored with the idea all morning. She had never seen it herself, not even from a distance. She knew it was there, across the gully on the far end of The Suburbs in which she lived, but it was through clusters of neighborhoods Hannah had no reason to visit.

When her parents spoke of The City, they spoke as if the encroaching sprawl were made of cancer. That it was a blight. A fungus. A toxic waste spill. At best, an eyesore. At worst, a coffin. But Hannah didn't believe all that. Although she always pictured The City to be loud and smelly and crowded and dangerous, she also imagined it would be exciting. And interesting. And inspiring. And even beautiful, in its own weird way.

Mr. Mahogany resumed his lesson.

"Like the caterpillar becoming a butterfly, you too will emerge on the other side of your metamorphosis as your true adult form. Completely different, though exactly the same. The memories you carry into the FINAL TESTING ROOM will seem like distant fogs, spurious and abstract vapors that only served to incubate the eggs you all currently are..."

"What does it feel like?" a student in the back asked.

"I'm sorry?"

"The transformation," the student said. "Does it hurt?"

"I'm not going to lie to you kids," he addressed the class. "For most of you, the transition from meat to wood will not exactly be a pleasurable experience. Your body is a biological mechanism, and like all biology, it has a built-in defense system. And it will try to fight the change. But, ultimately, it will lose. The body, as resilient as it may be, also has many weaknesses. Flesh can be torn, abraded, cut, ripped. It can get infected. It can cause you pain. But once your strings are attached and the puppetfeed has worked its way through your system, the pain will subside. Any illness that may be hiding in your body – be they viral or bacterial - will be purged out. You will most likely pass out from the overwhelming nature of this sensation. Don't fight it. Let the sleep take you. When you awake next, you will have hopefully finished the maturation process..."

But Hannah didn't hear any of that.

Her teacher's words passed right through her head like a boxcar train on its way to some grander depot in the heart of a metropolis far away from this boring old classroom.

Six

Hannah was walking home after school.

She moved briskly. Mechanically. This was a familiar route, one she had traveled as far back as she could remember. She could sidestep these potholes even if she were blindfolded. The only difference she noticed as the days wore on were the cracks in the concrete beneath her feet. What years ago was only a hairline fissure had, in time, become a fully gouged-out chasm. And though it was only a few inches wide and a half an inch deep, Hannah liked to pretend it was a thousand-mile canyon. She liked to pretend she was a giant. That she could climb over anything.

The houses here all looked the same. Two story colonials, lined up like teeth. The safe, pastel suburbs, smiling at her.

As she plodded across the concrete sidewalk, her heels clicked against the pavement. One foot before the next. Her gait was even and her footsteps slowly began to take on a musical tone. Like a metronome. There was a beat, as if her toes were singing.

So she started to fill in the down notes. Double-stepping. Triple-stepping. Half-stepping. Skipping a step entirely. She settled into a pattern, a pleasing sequence of taps and pauses, a Morse-code of footwork only she could decipher.

She repeated it. Again. And again. And again. And her brain started to feel as though it were in a trance. She faded out of herself, disassociated from the arduous and pervasive thoughts that normally dominated her mind, and she became one with the flow. Movement had taken over. She exuded poetry. Her body was art.

She was dancing.

The strings coming out of the black voids above her seemed to vibrate for her. The whole world hummed like a medieval lute.

And as she danced, she started to wander. Not intentionally, but the music in her head was a zephyr and she was a feather and she had surrendered herself to the cadence of her own heart. She waltzed down a side street. A road on which she'd never traveled. She fandangoed a couple of more blocks, flamencoed a few more, before pirouetting into the neighborhood adjacent to that.

By the time she stopped dancing, she realized she had no idea where she was.

Hannah looked around. The houses here weren't quite as nice as what she was used to. Yards were smaller, closer together, full of junk. Where grass grew, it grew in unkempt patches, and where there was dirt, it was wet and muddy. The washed-out paint on one house was even completely peeling off. The house looked like it had a sunburn.

This part of town was ugly. Unfriendly. Not her home.

She walked down the road a while, until she came upon a small park. All the playground equipment was rusted. The slide like a razorblade. The swing set like a row of nooses.

A single set of strings came out of a nearby void. Like cobwebs they attached themselves to a man who sat facing away from her, slumped over, unmoving, on one of the park benches.

Hannah walked apprehensively across the park and approached him.

"Hello?" said Hannah.

The man did not respond. Puppetfeed oozed down the string stuck into the back of his head. The sound it made as it forced its way into his body was the same kind of squish a banana would make were it mashed between fingers.

"Excuse me," said Hannah as she got nearer. "I seem to have gotten myself turned around. I don't live around here.

I was wondering if you could point me in the direction of..."

She trailed off as she saw his face. Like the house down the road, his paint was chipping off too. She could see the untreated wood underneath. It was not the umber color of natural trees, but rather, a sickly mix of tan and gray, like a picnic table that had been left out in the rain for too many years. He didn't move. His expression was one of despondency. His gaze, were he lucid enough to be gazing in the first place, was pensively fixed to the ground by his feet. Hannah wasn't sure of what it was that had caused him to end up in such a state, but she felt, in equal parts, empathy and revulsion.

"Mister?" she said.

He didn't respond. Was he dead? Was this what puppets looked like when they died? She had never seen a dead body before. Puppets don't age, so death, in the natural sense, was not something she had ever encountered.

With trepidation, she extended one of her bony fingers and took another step towards the impotent man. And just as she was about to poke him in his cedar shoulder, his head suddenly jolted upright. Black eyes as wide as bocce balls rolled towards her. They seemed to glisten with the evening dew. Hannah could see herself reflected back in them. She looked terrified.

"Help me!" he cried out as his jaw fell laggardly open.

Hannah stumbled backwards and fell into the mud as the puppet man clattered to life. He hung clumsily by his strings, as if whoever were pulling them was too lazy to bother mimicking realistic movement. He lurched towards her in spasms, repeating the same terrifying phrase over and over again:

"Help me! Help me! Help me!"

Hannah crawled backwards, deeper into the mud. It soaked into her clothing and made her feel heavy. It was as if the mud was holding her there.

Woodpulp started to pour out of the man's mouth. Tiny flakes like dry oatmeal. The wind blew and it created a snowstorm of sawdust that twisted around the two of them like a cyclone. The woodpulp vomit became more profuse, moister, stickier, until his mouth couldn't handle the volume of it. One of his black eyes popped out of his head and plopped down into the dirt. More sawdust came pouring out of that hole.

"I don't know what is happening to me," he gasped through the pulpy dust erupting from every opening in his face.

He reached out to grab her. With all the strength her skinny body could muster, Hannah pulled her feet out of the mud and scrambled until she was able to stand.

And then she ran.

She ran and ran, without knowing where she was going. But still, she continued to run until she found the cracks in the sidewalk she was familiar with. Back on her route home from school. She bound over canyons. Each step propelled her forward, hundreds of miles at a time.

She ran until she was safe at home.

Seven

"Look at you! You're covered in filth! You're a disgrace! An absolute disgrace!"

Hannah had just slipped in through the front door and those were the first words her mompet had said to her. Her puppet mother was standing with her hands on her hips and had her eyebrows the ability to convey any complex emotions, they surely would've been bent upward in umbrage.

"I hope the neighbors didn't see you walking around like this," her mompet said as she peeked out from in between the curtains.

"The neighbors weren't outside," went Hannah.

"Well let's thank The Puppeteer for small miracles," her mother facetiously said. "I don't know how I'd explain to them the state you are in. My daughter, Queen of the Dirt. Where the hell were you?"

"Nowhere," said Hannah. "I was coming home from school. I got just lost."

"Lost?" said her mother. "Lost?! How can you get lost? You've walked back and forth to school a thousand times before."

"I know. I'm sorry, momma. I just went the wrong way today."

Her mom shook her head. "I don't know. I just don't know anymore, Hannah. Most kids your age are not getting into these sort of easily avoidable predicaments. They're at home doing their studies, showing up for dinner on time so they could grow big and strong, preparing for the transition into adulthood. If you were busy doing the things you were supposed to, you wouldn't be doing the things you're not.

This...*attitude* you have...this *insolence*...it's just not normal. It's almost like an insult, like you're throwing all the work we put into raising you right back in our faces. Aren't I right, dear?" she turned to Hannah's father for support.

Her dadpet jerked awake from his chair. "Listen to your mother," he said before returning to his crumpled state.

Hannah didn't tell her parents about the crazy man she had seen. About how he attacked her and how she fell backwards into the mud. She didn't tell them about all the weird things he was saying or how his face had exploded with bits of wet sawdust. It would've just been another argument Hannah was too exhausted to have.

"Just clean yourself up," her mother said, obviously exhausted too. "Take off those muddy clothes and come downstairs and eat. It's been dinnertime for over an hour."

Hannah did as she was told. She rinsed out her hair and put on a fresh dress. She walked down the creaky stairs in their dark and cavernous home and joined her parents at the dining room table.

Hannah sat there in the suffocating silence and ate her cold acorn mash. And in between bites she couldn't help but notice the sound of the puppetfeed being injected into her parents' heads was identical to the sound it made as it was coming out of that crazy man's body.

Eight

Hannah had hardly slept at all that night.

The image of that man's exploding face haunted the back of her eyelids. It polluted her. Made her feel sick to her stomach. It kept her awake as if it were an alarm clock that was blaring in her ear.

And the darkness of her bedroom seemed to expand. The ceiling bled black. It ran down her walls like pen ink, covering the posters of unicorns she had pasted up, each mythical creature disappearing underneath the ebony wave. The void distended like a water balloon until the weight of it started to suffocate her.

And her thoughts felt like truck tires. And her thoughts smelled like hot rubber. And her thoughts were just a shadow show on the blank walls of her imagination. And her thoughts were just more puppetry that she herself could not control.

And then it was morning and the light came in and all of the terror of the night was quietly forgotten.

Nine

Children filled up the hallway like rats in the gallows of a ship. The unavoidable stink of biology wafted off the student body as if they were the fumes from a tailpipe; a cyclone of salty sweat, dirty feet, and bad breath. The teachers couldn't smell it with their puppet noses. But Hannah and Jordan could.

"Jeez, this place smells like a butt," Jordan said, fanning the air in front of her nose. The two girls were pressed up against the wall by the entrance to the gymnasium. Kids shuffled by on their way to their next class. "It's like they're doing it on purpose. Like everyone is in some kind of contest to see who could stink the worst. Why do people smell so bad?"

"Bacteria," mumbled Hannah without thinking.

"What?"

She looked up at her friend.

"Um...well, bacteria is what causes body odor."

"What do you mean?" asked Jordan.

"They're everywhere," said Hannah. "Bacteria. They're all around you. They fill up your blood and cover your skin."

"What are you talking about?"

"Inside of you, right now, there are 10 times more bacterial cells than there are human cells. I read about it on the internet. They outnumber us. That means that even with all the thoughts and desires and needs and feelings crowding you up like the air in an overinflated balloon, 90% of what you consider 'you' is actually not you at all. It's them."

Jordan looked horrified.

"It could be argued that the whole reason you even exist

33

in the first place is to give the bacteria a vessel in which to thrive."

"That's so gross, Hannah," said Jordan. "Why do you know that? Why are you even *thinking* about that?"

Hannah shrugged.

"Whatever," said Jordan. "I'm certainly more than just a *vessel* for some nasty germs."

"You are," said Hannah. The she added, "But only 10% more."

A puppet teacher passed by. He stood taller than the rest of the kids, a sequoia tree amidst the shrubs. He eyeballed the two girls as he walked past them. They diverted their gazes down to their bellybuttons and waited for the teacher go away.

"What were you saying earlier? About last night?" asked Jordan. "You got attacked or something?"

"Yeah. Well, kinda. I don't know if he was attacking me or if he was just sick or what, but there was this...man in this park. He was just sitting there all slumped over. Like he was dead or something. When I went up to him he started coming at me and saying all this weird stuff."

"Weird stuff? Like what?"

"He kept screaming for help and then he said he didn't know what was happening to him."

"He didn't know what was happening to him? What does that even mean? What was happening to him?"

"I have no idea."

"So where was this?" asked Jordan.

"Some random park. I don't know what it was called. It was in some bad part of town."

"You went to a bad part of town?" said Jordan.

"Yeah, but it was an accident. I didn't mean to. I just was...I wasn't paying attention."

"That's so crazy."

"That's not even the weirdest part," said Hannah. "His

face was all messed up too. Like missing paint and stuff. And then he started throwing up this wet sawdust stuff all over the place. It was horrible. It was coming out of his mouth and nose and his eyes and everything. It was like he was exploding, from the inside."

"Puppets can't throw up," Jordan said, matter-of-factly.

"I know. But this one did."

"I want to check it out," said Jordan after a slight pause.

"Huh?" said Hannah.

"I want to check out this creepy park."

"I don't think that's a great idea," said Hannah. "My mom came down on me super hard yesterday when I showed up late."

"So we cut class the rest of the day and go there instead. That way, you can get home at the right time and your mom won't ever know you were out."

"Won't it be dangerous, though?"

"Nonsense," Jordan brushed off her friend's mounting concerns. "You're still alive, aren't ya? Plus, you're not going alone this time. We'll both be there. And nothing bad will happen if we stick together."

Ten

Hannah and Jordan made their way through the school, weaving around other students like river water around rocks. Had they yarn, their movements would've knit a quilt. Down a side hallway the two girls ducked, trying their hardest to remain invisible. They hid in corners like cockroaches and pressed against walls like the paint itself.

There was a particular room they passed by. It was down a dimly-lit and seldom-used hallway that branched off the main hall like a vestigial finger. The empty void that took up the ceiling above seemed to be even darker there, as if it were a version of black that could somehow be blacker. Blackest.

DO NOT ENTER – were the words written on the door – FINAL TESTING ROOM.

They were moving too quickly for her to be sure, but Hannah could've sworn she heard screams coming from inside.

Through a double set of fire doors they pushed and the two girls burst outside.

It was warm, but not hot. The sun hinted at the coming season, as if the summer were a secret it was still keeping to itself. The sky was blue and the grass was green and the brick-faced school stood behind them, a citadel amongst the gauze-like strips of parking lot and street.

The girls quickened their pace but were reeled back when a voice suddenly called out to them:

"Hey!"

They froze, eyes wide, and both and Hannah and Jordan pivoted on their heels, almost in unison.

Standing there was Hannah's kiss-ass younger cousin, Bette.

Hannah lowered her shoulders and let out a sigh. "Jeez, Bette, what are you doing here?"

"What are YOU doing here?" her cousin volleyed back.

"Nothing."

"I followed you because you were acting suspicious and I thought something was up," Bette said. "It looks to me like I was right. You're attempting to cut class, aren't you?"

Hannah and Jordan exchanged a nervous glance.

"Look, you're not going to tell on us, are you?" Hannah said.

"You shouldn't be cutting class," Bette said. "Especially this close to graduation. They're about to attach our stings and we should..."

"Bette, c'mon. Give us a break," said Hannah. "Can you stop being such a prig for once in your stupid life?"

Bette scowled. Hannah realized insulting her cousin might not have been the best move. Bette turned to reenter the building, but the fire doors had locked behind her. She jerked on the handles. The doors rattled, but did not budge.

"Shit," she nervously whispered to herself.

She turned back to face the young truants who were now closing in on her. She made a move for the front of the building but Hannah had gripped her by the shoulders.

"Be reasonable," said Hannah.

Bette diverted her gaze. "This is for your own good," she replied as she wiggled out of Hannah's grasp and started away from them towards the entrance. "I don't want to be a tattle-tale, but I have to help you if you can't help yourselves."

"Damn it, Bette!" shouted Hannah.

"Hey, why don't you come with us?" Jordan interrupted.

Bette froze. Stood there for a moment in contemplation before spinning around to face them once more.

"You want me to hang out...with you guys?" asked

Bette, her voice tinted crimson. She regarded them with a suspicious eyebrow.

Jordan gave Hannah an I-got-this nod.

"Yeah," said Jordan. "We were just going to this park."

"Just a park?" went Bette.

"Just a park," Jordan echoed.

"Listen, I..."

"It's so nice out today, isn't it? Wouldn't it be a nice day for the park?"

"But what about school?" said Bette. "I don't want to get in trouble."

"Well, I'm not going to tell on you," said Jordan. "Are you gonna tell on her, Hannah?"

"Nope," Hannah absently agreed.

"There you go," Jordan said. "We're the only two people who know you're out here, right? And our lips are sealed."

Bette thought about it for a few seconds more before the smallest hints of a smile started to creep across her cheeks. She walked back up to the girls.

"So where exactly is this place?" she asked.

Eleven

Hannah retraced her steps as best she could, but she wasn't drunk on dance like she was the last time so orientating herself was a difficult task. Now not even a foxtrot leapt from her heels. She plodded forward like her shoes were lead, her best friend and her cousin in tow.

"I don't think we should be over here," Bette nervously said as the neighborhood around them began to deteriorate. The other two girls ignored her whining although, at least in Hannah's case, she agreed. Arcadian facades slipped off the houses like Halloween masks after a night of trick-or-treating. The real face of the suburbs was far uglier than the sterile utopia it presented itself to be. In this neighborhood, Hannah didn't feel like a giant as she stepped over the cracks in the sidewalk. Here, she felt like a helpless little girl.

Eventually, they came across the park that Hannah had been at the day prior.

"This?" Jordan sneered. "This is it?"

"Well, yeah," said Hannah.

"It's not creepy at all. It's just old and shitty."

The park did seem a lot older and shittier than it had the day before. It was as if it had aged 10 years over night. Gnarled, brown vines had sprouted up from out of the mud and wrapped themselves around the chains of the swing set so that when the wind blew, it no longer rattled like the manacle around a prisoner's ankle. The sad merry-go-round appeared even less merry as the thick foliage choked its spokes.

Adding to this all was a newer, thicker black void that had settled just above the park. It blotted out the sun around them like the awning over a veranda. Hannah wondered how these vines grew so quickly and so strongly without receiving proper sunlight.

"And this is where you saw that dude?" asked Jordan, pointing to the nearby bench.

Hannah nodded. On the ground where he had vomited, a group of small vines grew, no taller than an inch or two each. It was almost as if he had thrown up fertilizer, but even fertilizer doesn't work that fast.

"What dude?" asked Bette. "What are you guys talking about? Are we supposed to be meeting someone here?"

"No," said Hannah. "Don't worry about it."

"I think you were seeing things, Hannah," said Jordan. "It's a possibility, right?"

"I wasn't seeing things," she quickly replied before contemplating it just a bit further. "At least, I don't think I was."

"I think we should head back. We're too close to The City," said Bette. "My mom and dad always warned me about The City. They said it was an unpredictable and dangerous place full of unpredictable and dangerous people. They said we have to stay on our side of town, at least until I become a puppet, then nothing can hurt me."

"Wait, we're close to The City?" Jordan's eyes lit up.

Bette looked at the position of the sun. "Um...I believe it should only be a few miles that way," she said pointing to the east.

"What the hell? These stupid houses around us are too tall," Jordan said. "I can't see anything over them."

She trudged into the muddy park trying to get a better view.

"Jordan, get back here," said Hannah. "You're gonna get dirt all over yourself."

But Jordan wasn't listening. She was sloughing through the muck. Hannah sighed and stepped in after her.

"Wait, don't leave me by myself," yipped Bette before

she begrudgingly followed them.

They slurped and popped across the mudfield like a row of asphodels across a sewer grate. For the amount of effort it took, it felt like it took hours just to move a couple feet. The vines seemed to grow in thicker with every step.

Jordan finally reached the rusty slide and climbed the rickety ladder to the top of it.

"I can almost see it," she shouted. "I can see the tops of the spires. And the antennas are poking up like kitchen knives. I just need a few inches more. Hannah, come up help me."

Hannah was at the bottom of the slide. "You should come down," she said.

"We're so close, Hannah. It's right there. Please. This is important. I want to see it."

Desperation was the ferry for Jordan's voice while her yearning like lemon juice squeezed its way out of her eyes. She didn't need to say another word, she didn't have to beg and plead because instinctually Hannah already knew. The look Jordan gave her could never be conveyed within the black plastic of puppet eyes. In that moment, it spoke volumes without speaking at all. And the makeup Jordan wore made her look like a movie star, adding to the dramatics of it all. It was so sincere, so agonizingly *human*, it was impossible for Hannah to say no. She climbed the ladder too.

Jordan used Hannah's shoulders to brace herself. She stood on her tippy-toes and craned her neck. Still, she couldn't see over the houses. So she climbed up Hannah's body like a flight of stairs. She stepped up onto her knobby knees, her bony hips, her sunken clavicle and finally, she stood on Hannah's face so the two girls were arranged on top of each other like a totem pole. Hannah tried not to move. Tried not to even breathe. Jordan's position was a precarious one, but she was finally tall enough to see The City.

"It's so beautiful!" Jordan cried out as one of her dirty

shoes slipped into Hannah's mouth. "The color! The lights! It's...it's...it's goddamn MAGICAL!"

"I want to see," said Hannah, reaching up. Jordan swatted her hand away.

"It just seems so ALIVE!" she gushed.

Then the slide started to shake. Lightly. It trembled like a cat left out in the rain. Its legs shook like it were a marathon runner at the end of a race.

"Be careful," Jordan said to Hannah.

"That wasn't me," Hannah replied.

"Um...guys..." said an apprehensive Bette from down on the ground.

"Not now," Hannah shouted to her cousin, her voice muffled by the rubber sole of Jordan's sneaker currently pressed up against her lips. "Can't you see we're busy?"

The slide shook some more. A bit more vigorously. Jordan almost toppled over.

"No, seriously you guys, there's something..." Bette repeated herself.

"Bette! Seriously, shut up," Hannah once again snapped.

"GUYS!" the 11-year-old suddenly cried out in terror.

Hannah finally looked down to see Bette being pulled into the mud. Thick, crusty vines had wrapped themselves around her legs and arms while smaller ones climbed up her skin in spider web patterns.

The vines also wrapped around the base of the slide and were pulling it downward too. They were sinking. Hannah gasped, but Jordan still wouldn't take her eyes off The City.

More vines came up from the ground. Dozens of them. Like living corn stalks. Like there were an ocean of octopuses underneath the ground trying their hardest to dig their way out. They reached upwards, whipping around like lassos, looking for anything substantial to grab onto. Some latched onto the playground equipment. Others merely reached upwards towards the black void above like an infant looking for an embrace from its parent.

Bette was dragged knee-deep into the mire. She screamed. She screamed until her voice was hoarse and the meat that lined her throat was expelled in her breath.

The swings were torn from the set. The sandbox was upended. The seesaw went perpendicular. The slide tilted so far forward that Hannah could no longer keep her balance. She fell over.

Jordan, who was in rapturous awe just moments before, now spilled forward too and smashed headfirst against the jagged side of the railing. It cut into her face; a deep sideways gash that went from her forehead, over her eye, across her nose, before ultimately ending at the cleft of her chin. Blood cascaded out of the wound like maple syrup. She clutched it in her palms. More blood oozed from between the cracks in her fingers.

In the mud they both landed with a splat. Immediately vines punched through the muck and seized them. One wrapped around Hannah's neck and squeezed. She gasped for breath as it pulled her entire head under the ground. Beneath the mud, there was no oxygen to be found, just the irreversible cold of the soil around her. A stillness and a silence overcame her as her body went numb. Her brain felt far away and the world felt fuzzy. And as her ears dipped down into the brown slime, she could hear voices talking. There were voices inside the dirt. Voices of people. They begged her to get them out of the soil. Tortured voices, desperate and pleading. When she didn't respond, their tone changed. They grew sinister. Viscous. Moist. They got angry and called her obscene names. They called her a whore. They told her she knew nothing. They told her there was no escaping them. That sooner or later, she would either become one of them, or become their lunch. This sensation was too great, the ground was too heavy. And the deeper she went, the louder and angrier the voices got.

It took all the strength she could conjure, but Hannah jerked upward until her back started to burn. Eventually, she pulled her face free from dirt. She flailed and jerked and moved in a spastic fit, unpredictable and peculiar, as more vines coiled around her waist and tried to pull her down. She tore them off, slipped out, snapped them in half. She broke free and crawled over to Bette and attempted to claw them off her too. Bette was sunken up to her waist. She wrapped her arms around her cousin's body.

"Hannah!" she cried. Hannah braced herself and strained, but to no avail. As hard as she pulled up, the vines seemed to pull in equal part back down. They were mocking her effort. They were stronger than her, and they knew it. It didn't matter what she did. They were always going to be stronger. In a desperate and final move, and with little recourse left, Hannah leaned in and bit into the thickest vine wrapped around Bette's neck. She sunk her teeth deep into it. Blood came out of the plant. Crimson blood, thicker than paint. Hannah could taste it on her tongue. The sticky flavor of copper and salt. She gnawed until the vine severed and snapped. The tentacles reeled back and released Bette. Hannah yanked her out the mud.

"They can be cut," Hannah called out to Jordan.

Hannah trudged over to her friend. Jordan struggled and screamed and bled and sank. A muscly vine was wrapped around her waist, sucking her back-first into the swamp.

Hannah fell to her knees and chewed through the herbal umbilical cord. It snapped. Like a firehose out of control, the wounded aorta drenched them all with its ruddy earthgore.

The ground became even muddier and slipperier with the surging gore. It was as if they were in a giant stomach that was trying to digest them. But the three of them grouped up and sallied forward, pushing through the slough until they reached the sidewalk on the other side. They collapsed in a pile on the pavement. Beaten and bruised and out-of-breath.

"Help!" Hannah cried out as loud as she could. Jordan's face continued to spurt blood from the wound, her complexion going white. "Someone help us! Please help us! Anyone?"

She looked around. No one answered her. Not even the wind blew. In fact, the only signs of life she saw was a puppet in the picture window of one of the nearby houses, slowly pulling closed the shades.

Twelve

The dining room was a coffin.

The light in here felt fake. Like it was just more darkness masquerading as light.

Hannah had made it into the house on time and was able to clean herself up before her parents noticed. She wore a long sleeve sweater to hide the lacerations and bruises that ran up and down her arms.

She didn't eat her acorn mash. She was tired and hungry, but she didn't want acorn mash. She wanted flavors she never tasted, consistencies she'd never felt. But foods like that didn't exist, so she piled the gray gruel up into the shape of a mountain just so she could destroy it with her spoon and pile it up again.

"So how was school today?" her mother said, popping to life.

"Good," Hannah laconically replied.

"Good?" her mother scoffed. "That's all you have for me? Good?"

"What do you want me to say?"

Her mother sighs. "You want to know something? Every morning, when I wake up, I say a little prayer for you. I pray that you'll *evolve* out of this funk you seem intent on making us all suffer through. Life doesn't have to be as hard as you make it, Hannah."

"School was good, Mom. I have nothing to say about it. It's the same thing every day."

"I feel sorry for you if you can't find any comfort in that," her mompet said. "You know I only ask because I care. I care. I care. I care. I care. I care. I care. I care." She began to nod and shake violently. "I care. I ca- I ca- I ca- I ca- I ca- Ca-ca-ca-ca-ca-ca-ca-ca..."

"Mom?" went Hannah.

"Yes dear?" her mother replied, returning to normal.

"You were just repeating yourself."

"Was I?"

"...yes?"

"Oh. I hadn't noticed."

"Are you...feeling alright?" Hannah asked.

"Of course," said her mompet. "Why do you ask?"

"Because you were just repeating yourself!"

"Was I?"

"YES!"

"Oh. I hadn't noticed."

The telephone rang in the other room and broke the loop they had somehow found themselves in. Her mother stood up and walked out to answer it. Hannah's father sat motionless across from her, as lively as an unloved toy. Though his strings remained unknotted he lay there with the barren languish of firewood.

"Was it ever this difficult for you?" she futilely asked him.

He didn't move. His head didn't even tilt towards her. But his jaw creaked open as he nebbishly replied, "Listen to your mother."

Plop replied the dollop of acorn mash that she let slide off the end of her spoon.

Her mother then reentered the room. Her wooden feet smacked against the floor. There was a swiftness in her step as she walked up next to her daughter. Her mother stood tall. Her strings were taut and the disapproving look that was permanently painted on her face was clear in the sickly light of the pallid chandelier.

"Those were your cousin Bette's parents," her mother fumed. Were she a dog, her voice would've come out as a growl. Were she a cloud, she would've spoken like thunder. "Now I'm going to ask you one more time, Hannah. How – was – school - today?"

Thirteen

Hannah was sent to her room.

Her mother was incensed. She lectured her daughter without periods or commas, her sentences an avalanche of words that spilled out of her mouth as if the hinges on her jaw had totally snapped off. Hannah couldn't even interject a simple 'but' before it was engulfed by the fury of her mompet's machinegun judgement.

But Hannah's mother had no clue as to how scared Hannah had been. She didn't know about the voices under the dirt. She had no idea that Hannah had risked her own life to pull Bette out of the mud and drag her back to the sidewalk. About how she gave up her own socks and used them to stop the bleeding on Jordan's face. About how she led the girls home all by herself, navigating the treacherous end of The Suburbs like a seasoned cartographer setting sail across the sea. Her mother didn't know any of that. Hannah's acts of bravery and heroism had been far overshadowed by the sin of her curiosity.

"...and to exploit your cousin's naïveté like that? You could've gotten her killed! Or ruined her entire life! You know, I sometimes feel bad for her, having to deal with you and that little friend of yours. What's her name? Jordan? Bette would be just fine without you or your subversion. I know it wasn't *her* idea to cut class. *She* does what her mompet tells her to. That's why she skipped two grades and why you're...well..."

Her mother sighed.

"Being obstinate is not a virtue, Hannah. These things that you value, this ineffectual rebellion and the hostility it

49

brings...it's all just empty. When you're my age, when you look back, you'll see. Once you attach your strings, all of this will go away and you and I can finally build a relationship. A *REAL* relationship," she said. "Friday can't come soon enough."

After her mom left, Hannah laid on her back on her bed. Her tears were hot, boiled by frustration. The black void of her ceiling looked down on her like an unblinking eye. In that moment, she hated everything. She hated the universe. She hated the parade of circumstances and coincidences that had led to her existence. She hated history, in its entirety, pressing its weight against this moment, right here. Why must she suffer when all it would've took was one missed coupling of DNA, one disease, one failed relationship, one turn down a different street, and she wouldn't have been here at all. She wouldn't have had to worry about anything. She wouldn't have been born.

The blackness above her was deep. Eternal and hollow.

Then there was a flash.

A small flash. Somewhere up there. Far away, inside the void.

She suddenly sat up and squinted through her tears into the hole above her. She definitely saw something. Or, at least, she thought she did. A light, a tiny little light like the aperture in a pinhole camera. It flared, twinkled for a few seconds, as if mocking the darkness, but by the next time Hannah blinked it was already gone.

Once again, Hannah thought of the trillions of bacteria living inside of her. She wondered if the creatures inside the microscopic universe of her body were going through similar turmoil. Or if her sadness affected them. Were they unhappy when she was unhappy? Did she create their weather?

This made her feel worse. There were so many of them. Colonies and continents beyond her sight. And they were all counting on her.

So she did what she could. She ran her fingers through her hair and pulled out the tangled flakes of rust that had come off the slide. She placed them on her tongue. The taste of iron was so strong it sent electric chills through her blood. But she chewed it up and swallowed it. She got on her hands and knees and licked up the dust and filth that had collected up in the corners of her room. She ran her finger through the mold that was growing just outside her windowsill before putting the slimy fungus in her mouth. It made her gag, but she swallowed it anyway because Hannah vowed to be a better mother to the diseases than her mother was to her.

Fourteen

The ticking of a clock. Impartial and cold.

Time is the dirge that encompasses all instruments. It is a funeral procession that stretches on without end. It will bulldoze every mountain, fill in every valley, it will march down every street and knock on every door. Each second that passed by was but the echo of an eternal gong; a stark and constant reminder of a countdown that began long before they were born.

Hannah stared at the man and he stared right back at her and the weight of their silence grew heavier for them both as the hands on the clock continued to move forward.

"Ya know, we can sit here all day," Dr. Alder finally said. "I get paid either way."

Painted on his barrel-round chest was an ivory colored suit, detailed with ribbons of blue and gold. He wore only the finest acrylics. His cheeks were just the right amount rosy, simulating natural flesh without veering into parody. His teeth were immaculately crafted and placed in his jaw evenly. His hair, though thin, seemed soft and natural, perhaps taken from a wild horse. And although his eyes were as black as any puppet's eyes, there was an affability about them that put Hannah at ease, despite her best efforts to remain angry.

"I don't know..." she trailed off.

"You don't know what?" asked Dr. Alder.

"I don't know why my mother made me come here," she said.

The counselor let out a light chuckle.

"Fair enough," he said. "But the thing is, I don't know why you're here either. Your mom wanted me to talk to you. She thinks you might be having problems adjusting at school. But I don't know any of the details. Sure, I could've gotten them from her if I wanted to, but I would rather hear them from you."

The counselor's office was spacious. In the corner sat his desk, but both he and Hannah were seated in large, plushy chairs by the picture window. Sunlight reflected off the white walls which made it seem more airy than clinical. They had even put up tiles to cover the black void in the ceiling, leaving only a thin track from the front of the office to the back for Dr. Alder's strings to come through.

"My mother keeps telling me that I'm going to be miserable unless I start taking my graduation seriously."

"Well attaching your strings is a very big deal," said the doctor. "It is, perhaps, the most important thing you'll ever do. Do you think that justifies her concern?"

"I guess," Hannah tersely replied. "But if it's so important, I don't understand why I'm being *forced* to do it. Why can't I take my time? Figure things out?"

"But you've already been afforded that luxury, Hannah," Dr. Alder said. "You've been given time to figure things out. You got to be a child. Nobody denied you that."

"But it wasn't enough," she said.

"It doesn't matter. That's all the time you get."

She frowned. "Things have just been really weird lately..."

"Weird, eh?" he said. "Well, adolescence is a time of change. The transition into adulthood is never easy. Things are bound to feel a bit different than they used to."

"I know," said Hannah. "But it's more than that."

"So why don't you tell me what you mean when you say that then?" he said. "What, exactly, do you mean by 'weird'?"

She paused for a moment.

"Well," she said, "Last night, before she got angry at me,

my mompet was broken for a moment."

"Broken?"

"Yeah. Or at least that's how it seemed. She started repeating herself."

"Well, were you listening to her?" he said.

"She kept saying 'I care' over and over again. Like dozens of times. Same exact words with the same exact inflection."

"It sounds to me like she cares," he said.

"You don't find that odd?"

"Odd that your mother cares?"

"That she would repeat herself like that. It was like she was trapped. Or short circuiting. Or something. It was like there was something going wrong *inside* of her."

"I don't really know your mother," he said. "But I'm sure she had a perfectly reasonable excuse for repeating herself dozens of times."

"And then there was the park..."

"Tell me about the park."

"I had gotten lost the other day. On my way home from school. I was dancing. I like to dance. I ended up at this park in an ugly part of town and there was a man there. An adult. But he didn't look like right. Like he was sick or something. He was missing part of the paint on his face, and when I went to approach him he started moving around all strange. All jerky, like his strings were tangled somewhere up where I couldn't see. When I tried to run, all this...*stuff* started pouring out of his mouth. When we returned the next day with my friend and my cousin, these vines came out of the mud and tried to drown us. And I heard voices under the dirt. They cursed at me and told me that I didn't know anything."

"There were voices in the dirt?"

"Yes."

"And he was getting sick?"

"Yes."

"Puppets don't get sick, though," Dr. Alder flatly said.

"Yeah but..."

"Hannah, this is a fact of life," he curtly said. "Puppets don't get sick. They don't throw up or act 'weird' as you put it. And I can assure you there is nothing under the dirt that doesn't belong there."

"I know," said Hannah. "I'm just telling you what happened. What I saw."

"So why are you lying to me?" he said. His head had begun to shudder and twitch as if he were shooing away a gnat. The tremors traveled past his shoulders, down the carefully carved balls that connected his joints, and then out the ends of all four of his limbs. They moved like weather vanes answering to four different winds.

"Wait, what?"

"Why are you such a filthy little liar?" he said as his formerly good-natured timbre suddenly disappeared. Now every word he spoke sounded if it were filtered through a screen of phlegm. Acrid and virulent, like something was caught in his throat.

Hannah's mouth hung open. "But..."

"I don't know what you think you have to gain by coming in here and wasting my time with your stupid made-up stories, but it ends now," Dr. Alder growled through his clenched teeth.

"I'm – I'm not making this up," Hannah pleaded.

The counselor awkwardly and unevenly rose to his feet. He was an imposing man, thick and proportional, possibly part redwood or Sitka spruce. As he stood the sunlight seemed to shrink around him. Hannah felt like a pearl trapped in the oyster's mouth. She sunk in her chair as she was engulfed by his massive shadow.

"Hannnaahhhh," he moaned with a voice like a wet paper towel. "You really don't know anythinggggg..."

He lunged towards her. She yelped and rolled out of the way. She hit the floor before scrambling back to her feet and strategically placed a chair between them.

"Dr. Alder?" she said through hyperventilated gasps. "What are you doing? What is happening?"

The counselor hobbled towards her as if he were drunk. His body jangled like a basket of vipers. He lowered his jaw on its squeaky hinges and let out a guttural shriek. Hannah could feel it cleave right through her fragile skin and bore deep into her bones.

Sawdust began pouring out of Dr. Alder's open mouth. Just a few flakes a first. Like ticker tape. But soon it grew pulpy and moist. It poured out thicker than pudding and splattered against the thin carpet around Hannah's feet in a beige puddle.

Mixed into the sawdust were worms. Grubs. Little white larva wiggling around in torturous fits. They blindly squirmed in every direction like a paddy of living rice.

He grabbed the chair and threw it against the wall. It smashed into a crystalline lamp and they both shattered. His jaw snapped completely off. A deluge of woodpulp poured from his face.

Hannah backed away slowly trying to keep him at a distance, but he kept following her with a ragged step to match every one of her own. Ceiling tiles fell away as he moved off the track, revealing the black void that rested above them. And as if the veil of the void seeped down into the room, its dark light corrupted everything it touched. What was sinister seemed even more sinister. What was bleak seemed bleaker still.

Hannah was cornered. Adrenaline surged through her veins like fire. Her breathing felt arrested. Lungs pumped in fits. Her mouth gone dry like her tongue were made of a sock. Panic so palpable it felt like physical hands wrapped around her throat.

And Dr. Alder loomed over her. The sawdust surrounded him like wasps. His face had been stripped of features as if he had been rubbed by sandpaper. He stood as the vertex of this onslaught; disaster in every direction like octopus tentacles around him. And right before his bulk completely consumed her vision, right before his body descended on her like a zeppelin, right before he finally seized her and destroyed her in his great swooping arms, a bell rang out.

ding

He stopped. Everything seemed to stop. Even the thousands of scabs of sawdust stopped, suspended in the air. Everything hung for a moment, giving Hannah just enough time to peek out of one eye and behold the room like a Polaroid picture, stock-still in the midst of the former chaos.

And then, without warning, his strings went taut and Dr. Alder was yanked up into the void. His body ragdolled by the force, but he didn't make a sound. His flaccid wooden frame was pulled into the darkness almost as fast as it took to blink and before a second passed, he was nothing but a tiny speck in the deepest parts of space.

But it wasn't just the counselor who was consumed by the darkness. The sawdust went with him. And the little worm-like creatures in it like a swarm of bees flying straight up at a thousand miles per hour. The furniture was sucked up there too. Broken chairs and shattered lamps and even Dr. Alder's entire desk which sustained only a scrape during the melee. All the books with torn pages, all the fibers of carpet that were stained by sweat and puppet puke. In a whirlwind it was all sucked into the hole in the ceiling, rocketing straight up until it disappeared.

Hannah stood up and nervously peered into the void. She had never seen anything like that before. She looked towards the exit, but before she could leave the room, a desk came down from the void like a comet. It came roaring back into the office like it were ready to obliterate the building, but for whatever reason right before it slammed into the ground, it landed gently where the counselor's desk had been before.

Then came the rest of his things: the books, the lamps, the patches of carpet, the chair. Hannah put her hands over her head to protect herself. It was raining furniture, except everything landed exactly where and how it had been when Hannah first entered the office. The chairs were repaired. The books rebound. The carpet cleaned.

And then, lowered in on strings from the heart of the sky came Dr. Alder himself. He hung limp, as if a corpse. Unlike the desk and chairs, he was not thrown back into the office, but gently, carefully, placed back in the chair he had sat at earlier in Hannah's session. His face and suit had been completely restored. His warm cheeks had been repainted. Every dapper hair on his head had been replaced.

Everything was completely back to normal.

And for a protracted moment, there was total silence, save for the metronomic ticking of that unsympathetic clock.

Dr. Alder snapped back into consciousness. Looked at the expired timer. Cleared his throat.

"Well then, Hannah," he said with as much of a smile as a puppet could muster. "Looks like our time is up."

Fifteen

Hannah sat in class.

Her hair was combed and her shoelaces were tied and her blouse had no wrinkles and her schoolbook was open to the proper page and she faced-forward like everyone else in the room.

But inside her head, her thoughts felt like pinballs in a machine. Her brain was tilted sideways. She was hemorrhaging quarters.

There was something very wrong with the world and she seemed to be the only one to know it.

She regarded Mr. Mahogany with little attention as he once again prattled on and on and on and on about what to expect at 'graduation'. It was another useless lecture. More wasted breath. Hannah already knew what to expect. Not only had her teacher talked about this a dozen times before, but she had also seen it played out in the movies and on TV throughout her entire life.

The students donned polyester robes, all sitting on fold-out chairs in an auditorium. Their puppet parents in the bleachers painted in their semi-formal best; restaurant attire. There were administrator speeches, rhapsodized talk of the sanitized and pain-free 'future' in which the graduates were about to embark. There were diplomas given. Cheers cheered. Hats thrown high into the air. And then they will form a single-file line, winding its way around the school. And one by one they will be led down the hallway, into the FINAL TESTING ROOM. And there they will be strapped to a chair. And a teacher will perform the procedure that permanently attaches the strings to their bodies. And then the puppetfeed will enter their bloodstreams and the transition will occur. And then they will come out the other end, completely transformed into wooden puppets.

It wasn't rocket science. It was perfectly natural.

Jordan wasn't in class that day. She didn't show up the day before either. Hannah hadn't seen nor spoke to her since the incident at the playground. Her desk remained empty on the other side of the room.

Hannah had tried telling her mother about what happened in Dr. Alder's office. About how he suddenly began acting strangely. About how he attacked her. About the grubs wiggling around in his vomit. And how he was sucked up into the void and replaced by a newer, cleaner version of himself. But her mother didn't believe her. Once again she was scolded for making up stories. Hannah didn't press the issue any further.

The bell rang.

"Hannah," Mr. Mahogany said over the chorus of slammed books and sneaker scuffs, "Would you mind hanging back a second. I'd like to have a word with you. Privately."

The rest of the students collected their belongings and left. Hannah stood there until it was just the two of them alone in the classroom.

"Why don't you have a seat," he said, motioning to the closest desk.

Hannah slid into the chair. Mr. Mahogany stared at her. They didn't speak for a moment. The teacher paced around, his clogs lightly clomping against the tile floor.

"One day..." he finally said.

"One day?" Hannah echoed.

"In one day's time you are going to graduate and we are going to attach your strings."

Hannah raised an eyebrow and sheepishly shrugged.

"I'm worried about you," he said.

"You are?"

"Well, maybe 'worried' isn't the right word. But rather... disturbed."

"Disturbed, Mr. Mahogany? There's no reason for that," she said. "I'm perfectly normal. Everything is perfectly normal."

Hannah tried her best to sound convincing, though she knew her voice was wavering like a flag caught in the breeze.

Mr. Mahogany sighed.

"You just don't exactly seem ready for the change," he said.

"That's what I've been telling people!" Hannah gasped. "I don't think so either, but no one wants to listen to me."

He picked up an apple a student had left on his desk. Puppets had no need for apples so he threw it in the trash.

"The thing is, the world isn't going to afford you any more leeway than you've already taken," he said. "You have to understand, I didn't create the universe. I have no providence over it. Both you and I know this is going to happen tomorrow, whether you like it or not."

Hannah looked down, a slight stamp of defeat in her gaze.

"I know," she mumbled. "But..."

"The thing is, I must insure this happens tomorrow. We've been watching you, Hannah. We see you trying to subvert the system," he cut her off. "Assert yourself. A wrecking ball of hollow rebellion. That is not how this works. Your biology is our fate. We cannot let you undermine our efforts. Not when we're this close..."

She looked up at her teacher.

"We?"

"Arrogant child," Mr. Mahogany said, his voice full of mud and gravel. "You think you know so much. But you know nothing. Nothing of the world or how it *truly* works. Nothing about the dirt and all that thrives underneath. We are coming. We are coming."

He slowly opened his mouth so wide that the top part of his head fell backwards, attached to his jaw like a barn door. Hannah could see all the way down his throat. To her surprise, there was a hole there. An actual esophagus, like on an animal. It even seemed to be fleshy, packed with swollen red corpuscles and fluffy white fat.

Hannah was both sickened and confused. Puppets don't have throats. And they certainly don't have any meat in them.

He leaned in closer. From inside his throat hole he continued to speak in garbled spurts and wet spats, bypassing the movement of his mouth altogether, and a chorus of whispery voices all talking in unison came out from the inside of his neck.

"It's time to stop making waves, Hannah. Submit and everything will be okay. Okay. Okay. Okay. Okay. Okay. Okay. Everything will be okay in the end. Give up. You just have to relax. Relax. Relax. And let the process take over. Process. Take over. And give up. Give up. Relax."

He jerked his head forward and it snapped shut. He looked at her with his marble eyes. There was an intensity in there. An air of austerity. Something in there that burned like fire but without any light.

"You understand, yes?"

Hannah nodded yes.

"Good. Now get out of here. I'll see you tomorrow at graduation."

Hannah grabbed her books and quickly ran out of the classroom.

Sixteen

"Bette! Hey, Bette! Wait up!"

Hannah called out to her cousin from across the crowded hallway.

Students filled the school like salmon in a stream. Bette turned around and saw Hannah poking her head up like a stone in the center of a whitewater river. She didn't answer her back. Instead she slammed her locker shut and quickly disappeared into the crowd.

"Damn it, Bette," Hannah mumbled to herself before starting in after her.

Immediately, she was pressed between bodies. Warm and smelly and sticky with sweat. Hannah pushed her way through the students like an Amazonian explorer pushed their way through the brush. For whatever reason, she was having flashbacks of the living vines in the park.

"Bette?" she cried out.

"Stay away from me, Hannah," her cousin called back.

"I just need to talk to you," Hannah said. "I need to talk about what happened the other day. I need to talk about what's happening..."

"I don't have anything to say to you," Bette's voice rang out above the din.

"There's something going on," Hannah said. "Something big. It's like the puppets are getting sick. Or going crazy. Or SOMETHING. There's something happening to them. I don't know what it is but I think it has to do with what happened to us at the park the other day."

Hannah pushed aside students in search of her cousin. She burrowed through the throngs like a human gopher. But for every person she shouldered past, two more seemed to pop up in the way. It was almost as if they were dividing. Splitting. Undergoing mitosis. It was almost like they were the germs that coursed through Hannah's own body blown up to human size.

"Bette?" Hannah called out. "Bette, where are you?"

But Bette had completely disappeared into the crowd.

Seventeen

Fingers like swamp reeds. Like raindrops against a rooftop. The pitter-patter of her knotty knuckles as they danced across the door.

Moments later, Jordan's mom answered with one shoe on and half of her synthetic hair up in curlers.

"Oh, hi, Hannah," she said.

Jordan's mom always seemed to be running late for something. Hannah's mother had told her it was because when Jordan's mom was young, she didn't eat all her acorn mash. She said Jordan's mom was a troublemaker and didn't pay any attention to her studies in school. Hannah's mother had told her that Jordan's mompet was one of the last kids in her class to graduate and by the time the teachers were supposed to attach her strings, they didn't do a very good job and left her brain all tangled up in knots. Hannah's mother liked to use Jordan's mom as an example, a this-could-happen-to-you-if-you-don't-do-what-I-say kind of cautionary tale.

"Is Jordan home?" asked Hannah.

"Is she?" thought Jordan's mom. "Yeah. I believe she's in her room. Come on in."

Hannah entered.

Jordan's house was a lot smaller than hers. Hannah's house was cold and cavernous. Jordan's house seemed... claustrophobic. The living room was always a mess. They didn't eat dinner in the dining room. Hannah didn't even know if they had a dining room. There were crusty plates and cups on end tables and old newspapers piled up against the foot of the couch.

"School good?" asked Jordan's mom while slipping on her other shoe.

"School's fine," Hannah obligatorily replied.

"That's good," she said. "School is important. The world is built to help those who help themselves."

Jordan's mom was never married. She had had a bunch of boyfriends over the years. All different types of guys, from businessmen to trash collectors to everyone in between. Hannah had met a few of them before. Some were pretty cool. Others were complete jerks. The only thing that all these men had in common is they never stuck around for too long. If Jordan's mom had a heart, it would've probably turned to wood anyway. She was flustered and sad and always seemed to be searching for something.

"Well I'm off to work," she said. "Tell Jordan there's $10 on the table for dinner. You girls have fun."

And she left.

Hannah made her way down the dim-lit hall.

"Jordan?" she said, pushing open the door to Jordan's bedroom.

It was dark. Darker than just the sable light cast by the void above. It was lampless. Dark as the ink of a squid.

"Jordan?" Hannah repeated herself.

The cherry tip of a lit cigarette cut through the twilight like a flaming sword. A pumpkin of light. Jordan inhaled and Hannah could barely make out the shape of her in the cigarette's orange halo.

"Jordan?" said Hannah. "What are you doing in the dark?"

Jordan exhaled dramatically.

"Nothing," she said. "Absolutely nothing."

"You weren't in school today."

"I didn't feel well."

"You're sick?"

"No."

"I'm going to turn on the light."

"If you must."

Hannah blindly ran her hand along the wall until she found the switch. She flicked it on.

Jordan sat in a chair at the far end of the room. A cloud of grey smoke surrounded her like the fog upon a bay. She stared blankly at the ground. Running from her hairline on the left, over one eye, across her nose and through the center of her now-bifurcated lips, all the way down to the bottom of her chin, was a scar. Thick and crusted, like a volcanic mountain range after an eruption. It protruded from her face and marred her entire countenance like a meat cleaver through beef. A jagged, ugly line that split her in two.

Hannah gasped.

"Don't act so startled, Hannah," Jordan said, taking another drag from her cigarette. "There's no monsters in the dark. Just me and you."

She offered Hannah a cigarette. Hannah refused, instead gawking at her friend's disfigurement.

"Your face..."

"...it's from when I fell off the slide," said Jordan. "Or, I should say, when you let me fall off the slide."

"Wait a second," went Hannah. "I didn't..."

"It wasn't that complicated, Hannah," said Jordan. "I trusted you. I trusted you to hold onto me."

Tears welled up in Jordan's eyes, which spilled over and ran sideways down the base of her scar, mixing with the beads of white pus leaking out from the edge of the wound. Such a beautiful bouquet of bacteria must exist in that vile discharge. Hannah, despite herself, couldn't help but wonder what it tasted like.

"Jordan..." she softly cooed.

"How am I supposed to be a model now?" she said. "I'm deformed!"

"Can I..."

"Look at me, Hannah. I'm damaged. Ruined. Everything I ever wanted is gone. I'll never be happy!"

"Jordan, if I could've helped..."

"If I had strings I wouldn't have fell," she somberly said. "If I was made of wood, I wouldn't have bled."

Her eyebrows defied the scar and curled malevolently as she redirected her scorn towards her remorseful friend.

"Get out," she growled.

"I can fix this," Hannah absently said. "I don't know how. But I can fix this. I can fix all of this. I can fix everything."

"Get out," Jordan repeated herself, yelling now. "Get out. Get out! GET OUT!"

Jordan threw a cup at Hannah. It hit the wall next to her head and shattered into a thousand pieces. Tears poured out of Jordan's eyes. Her makeup smeared like someone were trying to erase her but gave up halfway.

Without saying another word, Hannah left.

Eighteen

The afternoon was warm and there was no wind and the sun hung low like a Georgia peach on a lazy branch and as Hannah pushed her way out of her friend's house she wanted to scream.

Instead, she began walking.

She knew the direction she was headed, though not the destination. She walked with purpose, though she only had the vaguest idea of what that purpose might actually be. She felt confident, though it was completely hollow.

She didn't know exactly where she was going but she knew she wasn't going home.

She didn't leap and pirouette and tap her toes as she went. She didn't count the cracks in the sidewalk. She didn't even look down. She did not feel like a giant today. She was the size of a normal-person. She took normal-person steps as she walked away from the streets and neighborhoods she was most familiar with.

Hannah knew she shouldn't be headed where she was headed. Rationally, she knew what the consequences would be when her mother eventually found out. She knew exactly what her mompet would say, carefully cherrypicking her every vile word so that it cut her the deepest, felt the most caustic, hurt her the most.

Still, she couldn't help herself.

It was Hannah's willfulness that was and had always been the cause of all her problems. Her mother had made that clear, time and time again. If only Hannah had been born a little less Hannah, she probably wouldn't have had to feel so guilty all the time. If only the bacteria inside her guts made up 100% of her body instead of just 90%, she would've have had one less burden to bear.

Despite everything, there was still this compulsion inside of her. A need. An urgency. Undefined as it was, it felt to her as real as her arms. And it wasn't self-destruction. She was not trying to disappear. It was something else. Something more liberating than just anger. Something more profound than boilerplate sadness. She knew that once she became a puppet she would never see these streets again. Not in the same way. Not for what they really were.

She walked though she did not know what she was looking for, but she knew she wasn't going to find it in a classroom or at the bottom of a plate of acorn mash.

She walked past the park that had almost killed her and her friends a few days prior; the park that slashed up Jordan's face and tried to drown Bette in its dirt. By now, the mud had hardened over as if baked by the sun. It was just a flat, empty lot. As dead and as useless as any patch of pavement.

She walked across it and nothing happened.

Eyes watched from windows. The obsidian eyes of manikinkind. Almost alien. Like insects peering up from in between floorboards, they watched silently. Capriciously. Dissecting her lithe and human movements the way a science class might dissect a cockroach. But Hannah didn't care what they saw or what they thought. Not at this point. She had resolved to walk until she found an answer. A solution. Some sort of sign. Some sense of purpose.

Neighborhoods continued to decay around her. Soon the houses looked more like shacks. Plywood boards and graffitied bricks, hastily arranged, leaning up against one another like garbage in a landfill.

Dirty puppets wandered aimlessly about. Paint stripped from their weatherworn faces so that they lacked any recognizable expressions. They were emotionless. Blank. Like they were wearing masks. Some of these puppets were missing body parts: hands, arms, and legs. Others were even missing their feeding strings. Their wood was twig thin. Fungus attached itself to bodies, mushrooms like a pox sucking out what little nutrients might've been left in their balsa bones.

Some of these puppets eyeballed Hannah with suspicion, but most went about their business, oblivious to anything outside of their own miserable varnish.

She walked and walked and walked, until the streets ended and there was nowhere further to go. She had reached a railing. Comprised of iron and cast in evenly spaced bars that stretched from her left to her right, as far as she could see. It was as if the railing stretched all the way around the planet.

Ahead, on the other side of these bars, was The City.

She could see it more clearly than she ever had before. It seemed even bigger than she thought possible. Dozens of highrises poked up from the ground, almost as tall as the sky above them. The City called to her. All the gray concrete promise she had always imagined now stood there before her in all its bare-chested glory.

Jordan had been right though. Even at this distance, it still looked fake. Painted against the horizon.

Hannah was close, but not close enough. On the other side of the railing, separating The Suburbs from The City was a gully. It was wide, at least a mile across, completely flat, and stretched infinitely from one purview to the next. It looked like a dried-out riverbed.

And it was full of logs.

No water. No trees. Just endless rows of logs chaotically sprawled out amidst the patches of crispy yellow grass.

A puppet stepped up next to her. Hannah was startled but this puppet wasn't paying any attention to her. It just stood against the railing and looked out as if Hannah wasn't even there. It had no face. No clothes. She couldn't even tell if it was a man or a woman. It was just a blank figure made of hastily-sanded wood and pine-knotty joints.

Above the field was a singular massive void, the largest Hannah had ever seen. It was as if all the voids around her had bled together; an oil spill filling up the deepest trenches of the sky. And from the void came disembodied strings. Innumerable strings that were connected to nothing. They blew loose and wild in the wind. So many strings it seemed as if the void were just a Portuguese man-o-war quickly consuming the sea it once called its home.

Who did all these strings belong to? Hannah wondered, but she was not left to wonder for long, because as she followed them back down to the field she noticed the logs laying there in the gully were not actually logs at all.

They were corpses.

Puppet corpses.

Thousands of them, in different states of decomposition, sprawled out in all directions, filling up the ravine that divided The Suburbs and The City.

Many were posed as if they were trying to crawl across the grass and just didn't make it.

Hannah was horrified. Sickened. She didn't know puppets could even die. She had never heard of it happening before. Wood, when properly treated, should be able to last forever. That's what she had always been told. That was the whole POINT of becoming a puppet. But there it was in front of her. A genocide. A massacre. A grave as big as the horizon's berth.

Suddenly, the blank-faced puppet next to her jumped over the railing. It landed on the grass below with a soft thud. It stood for a moment, almost as if it were in awe of its own ability. Then it began running.

The puppet's legs and arms didn't work so well. It creaked like a haunted house as it moved. But still it sprinted as fast as it could towards The City. It leapt over the bodies of its fallen comrades.

Hannah watched as this addled puppet outstretched its crusty arms. It tilted its head up towards the void and ran as if it were expecting a big hug.

"I'm here," the puppet cried out to the darkness. "I'm here. I'm ready. Take me. Take me."

A tiny light once again momentarily sparkled in the center of the pitch, not unlike the one Hannah thought she saw in her bedroom the other night. And then, as suddenly as the puppet hopped the railing, all of its strings were violently ripped out of its back. In a spray of puppetfeed and splinters, the strings whipped around until they were indistinguishable from the myriad of other strings that hung from the void.

The running puppet's gait slowed down to a trot. It started to vomit the woodpulp the same way Dr. Alder had. It sprayed everywhere, like its face were a broken fire hydrant. And in the woody expulsion were grubs. A nestfull of grubs. They wiggled and writhed as they were scattered across the field.

The grubs immediately dug into the dirt as the puppet collapsed face down on the ground. Dead. And then, in the same spots the worms disappeared, vines punched their way out of the soil. Some even punched their way through a puppet's defunct body. Like biceps, they flexed their weedy muscles. And then they reached up too. Reached up towards the sky as if they were trying to grab ahold of those dangling strings and pull the whole void down on top of itself.

And then the vines grabbed onto the just-fallen puppet and entered its mouth and eyes and bore holes in its torso. The vines filled it up. The puppet convulsed. Jerked around like it were on fire. And then it stood up. It unnaturally rose on shaky legs and looked back towards the railing where Hannah stood.

Then it pointed at her.

"Soon," it said. "Soon, Hannah. Soon."

And in that moment, a feeling of hopelessness overcame Hannah. And the weight of this hopelessness was heavier than all the other emotions she had ever experienced combined. There were things at work in this world which she had not been privy to. Truths that had been obfuscated or hidden from her. Moments that were altogether too horrible to even name. And here they all were, presenting themselves to her, threatening her. It was as terrifying as it was pervasive and made her blood feel cold.

She was too small to fight this. Too weak to avoid it. Too helpless to even try. She wasn't sure what combination of words and action had initially set this whole terrible machine in motion, but these cogs were the size of cities. The size of moons. And they certainly didn't turn for her.

She vowed from that moment on to tread more carefully. To do what she was supposed to. Because, as she could clearly see, the alternative could be much, much worse.

No more insubordination. No more mouthing off. No more battling her mother tooth and nail over every pedantic detail of their inane lives. No more allowing her silly daydreams to build walls between herself and the world. It was time to do what she was told. It was time to grow up.

She was going to become a puppet.

And only fools dance.

Nineteen

Hannah went home and ate all her acorn mash. She shoveled that gray porridge into her mouth by the forkful and didn't think once about how much she hated how it felt all grainy in her mouth. Hannah ate all her acorn mash because that's what good girls are supposed to do when they sit down for dinner. And she wanted to be a good girl.

The silence of the dining room didn't even bother her. There was comfort in this silence. Familiarity.

"So are you excited about graduation tomorrow?" the habitual words leapt from her mother's wax berry lips, positing to her daughter the same question she had asked at every dinner for as far back as Hannah could remember, no matter how often or how vociferously Hannah protested.

But this time was different. Graduation was tomorrow. It was no longer some abstract event on some abstract date. This time, instead of talking back or arguing or making a big fuss, Hannah simply replied, "Yeah, Mom. I am."

Her mother froze for a moment. It was like the air had instantly turned amber, though Hannah kept breathing. Kept blinking. Kept eating her mash. Perhaps her mother had been expecting her to quarrel. But Hannah had no fight left to give. It was as if she were a dam that had suddenly burst. She had seen the things that lurked beneath the water and was drained of all resistance.

"That's good," her mom said, staring off into nowhere, nothing else to say.

Hannah finished the last bite of her dinner and laid down her fork.

"Hey, Mom?" she softly said.

"Yes dear?" her mother replied, turning her onyx gaze back to her daughter.

"I just wanted to say that I'm sorry," Hannah said.

"You're...sorry?"

"I know I've been kinda difficult to handle recently," she said. "I was just...afraid, ya know?"

"Afraid, honey?" her mother said. "What is there to be afraid of?"

"It's just...puppets aren't like people. Once you become a puppet, you don't change back."

"Life is a one-way ticket," her mompet said. "There's no escaping that."

"I was just lost for a moment, I suppose," Hannah said. "But I see now that I'm just a tiny branch on an endless tree that stretches out, forever and ever. If you think about it, this moment is the end result of history. Of evolution. Everything anyone has ever done, all their decisions, good and bad, have brought us here. I don't know why I was being so difficult. Fighting all that history."

"There's a naïve sort of certainty that comes with being a teenager," her mother said. "You discover the world and try to claim it as your own." Hannah's mother then pointed to her daughter's empty dinner plate. "You have not the perspective to see yourself as you truly are. Just an acorn amongst the oaks."

Hannah sighed.

"I guess what I'm really trying to say is I'm sorry, mama. I never meant to make you upset."

Her mother raised a cold cedar hand and placed it like a saddle on her daughter's trembling shoulder.

"It's all a natural part of growing up," she said. "You've hurt me, sure, but I never blamed you for that, dear. All vines must eventually push their way up through the ground, no matter how tough the soil may be. Had I a heart, there would be chambers in it that beat for you. All I can do, all I ever wanted to do, is what's best for you."

"And you know what that is?" asked Hannah. "You know what is best for me?"

"Of course I do," said her mompet.

Hannah smiled. "I love you, mama."

Hannah's mother was not physically able to smile back. Her stern expression had been painted on long ago. But she was able to move her nutcracker jaw, which fell open like a door to a cellar. And as her mother responded with equal and perfunctory affirmation, Hannah could almost swear that the voice coming from her mother's mouth emanated from somewhere deep down in her throat. Almost as if her voice actually came from inside her. Like her voice was charcoal in the furnace of her torso. Like it sat her belly, instead of her head.

She said back to her daughter:

"I love you, too."

Twenty

When her alarm clock went off the next morning, it didn't violently rip Hannah's sleep in two like it usually did. It didn't wail like an ambulance siren or bludgeon her into consciousness like the boxing glove of the dawn. Instead, the alarm aroused her with dulcet notes. It gently cajoled her out of bed. It told her a secret, whispered it in her ear, and for the first time Hannah could remember, she believed it.

Hannah got to school on time. Her hair was straightened and her low-heeled shoes were shiny. She was showered. Seraphic and spritely, as if she had shaken off all the anchors that had been holding her back. Today, she was the model student. Today, she was ready to become a woman.

The students were given black gowns and mortarboard hats. They were lined up and ushered into the gymnasium. They sat in foldout chairs that had been symmetrically arranged into two rows, with a thin aisle down the center. It looked just like it did in the movies.

Her parents sat in the bleachers with the other puppets. A tangle of strings came out of the void above and twisted up like electrical wires, like the mass of spectators were nothing more than a supercomputer.

Jordan was seated not too far away from Hannah. Just a couple of rows ahead. She wore an identical cap and gown. The diagonal scar that cut across her face had turned purple like the skin of an onion. Hannah tried waving, getting her friend's attention, but Jordan either didn't see her or was ignoring her. She faced forward and watched the ceremony with a scowl.

Administrators went up and said the things they're

supposed to say. The marching band weakly warbled out the school's fight song. A baby in the audience began to cry.

At one point Bette was called up to the podium. Her robes were festooned with more tassels and ribbons than everyone else. She was the valedictorian. She had to stand on a milk crate to be tall enough to talk into the microphone:

"The future may be unwritten, but it's not unclear. The path has been laid by you," she motioned to the parents in the bleachers, "And your parents before you, and their parents before them. Our tiny feet fit into your footprints as we follow you into the future. This is a tradition that I'm proud to be a part of. This is the culmination of years of hard work and determination, not just for me, but for all of us..."

When the ceremony was over, they threw their hats in the air.

Then they were organized into a single file line that went from the gym, weaved around the hallway, and lined up, one by one, in front of the room where their strings were to be attached.

It was time.

Twenty-One

The process wasn't going to be a gradual one. Nor was it going to be gentle. Hannah wasn't going to fall asleep a maggot and wake up a moth. This sort of transformation didn't take place over months in the privacy of her own personal cocoon. The metamorphosis from human being into puppet took a total of five minutes and it all happened behind the thick wooden door labeled DO NOT ENTER – FINAL TESTING ROOM.

Hannah was anxious, but not afraid. She thought of what laid just beyond the railing at the edge of town, of all those dead logs that had been felled in their attempt to reach The City. She had seen that there were far scarier things out there than acquiescing to normalcy.

She spotted her cousin standing a few places in line behind her. She waved to her.

"Bette. Hey, Bette. Could you come over here?"

Bette didn't move.

"C'mon," said Hannah. "Just for a second. I need to tell you something."

Bette rolled her eyes as hard as eyes can be rolled, but she eventually came over anyway.

"What?" she said.

"I just wanted to tell you that I liked your speech," Hannah said.

"Yeah, whatever."

"No, really," Hannah said. "It was good. It musta been nerve-racking to be up there in front of everyone. You're really smart and well-spoken. You made it seem easy."

"Oh," Bette replied, her voice softening a little. "Well,

thank you, I guess."

"Look, about earlier this week, at the park," said Hannah. "I'm sorry I dragged you out there. I'm sorry I went there myself, actually. I was just confused. I was angry at the world. I didn't mean to pull you into all that. You've always been a better kid than me. Smarter. Cuter. Just...better. I wasn't jealous or nothing like that, but I just knew that was never gonna be me, ya know? It just wasn't in the cards. But I'm not too proud to admit I was wrong about a lot of things or say that I'm sorry. So, I'm sorry."

Hannah finished talking and looked back up, half-expecting her cousin to be gone. But instead Bette stood there with a trembling lip. Her eyes were soft and watery. Before Hannah could say another word, Bette wrapped her arms around her and gave her a giant hug.

"You know I always looked up to you, Hannah," Bette said into her cousin's chest. "You were always so unapologetically you. So impetuous. So unafraid of everything. Even if it seemed misguided at times. I respected that. And deep down, on some primal level, I suspect I've always secretly wished I could be more like you."

Hannah hugged her cousin back.

And then the line inched forward.

And then it inched forward some more.

And the closer they got to the room, the darker the hallway seemed to get. The void that took up the ceiling was thicker here. Layers of darkness like sheets of fabric folded up in a linen closet. And from the room there was a noise. A noise unlike either of them had heard before. It wafted out from behind the closed door, traveled over the partition of the wall, and deposited itself into the ears of the two waiting girls. It was not a scream exactly, more like a sigh. But there was something sinister about it. Something unsettling.

Then the FINAL TESTING ROOM door opened and out walked Jordan.

The scar on her face had been sanded down and painted over. Her black hair was replaced with horse silk. Her slightly-awkward teenage proportions had been stretched to symmetry. She still looked as beautiful as she ever did. Maybe even more so. The minor imperfections that pocked her skin – the tiny blackheads and occasional blemishes - were all gone. And the strings that stuck up out of her hands and her legs and her shoulders and her head moved along with her.

"Jordan...?!" Hannah exclaimed with wide eyes.

"Hi I'm Jordan," her former friend said, holding out her hand for a handshake.

Apprehensively, Hannah took it. But instead of grabbing her block of a hand, there was something soft and slimy there. Hannah looked down and saw Jordan's hand had been replaced by the end of an insect. A grub. The wiggling butt-end of a worm wrapped around her wrist like a worm. It exuded warm mucus into her fingers.

"You don't remember me?" a confused Hannah said.

"Of course I do," said Jordan. "You are...you are...you are..."

"Hannah?" said Mrs. Balsa as she slowly reopened the TESTING ROOM door.

"Hannah," said Jordan. "You are Hannah."

"It's your turn," said the teacher as she motioned into the room.

"It's your turn, Hannah," Jordan echoed.

Hannah gave her cousin a nervous glance and then turned away from the other girls and entered the room.

Twenty-Two

The shadows here invaded her vision like soldiers marching through the night. Her sight was besieged. Dark patches had left their inky bootprints on the surface of everything. The void seeped down the walls. Every dusky corner seemed infinitely deep.

This was not a normal classroom. There was no blackboard up front and no desks in the back. There wasn't even a window by which Hannah would've stared out of and daydreamed on a normal day. The FINAL TESTING ROOM was a box, and it contained two things and two things only:

One was a machine that looked like something you might find in a hospital, a slow-beeping life support system that was peppered by a few dozen levers, monitors and knobs.

The other was a chair. A single chair that sat in the center of the room.

Mr. Mahogany stood next to the chair like a statue. A totem pole. His expressionless face gave Hannah no clues as to what to expect, no indication of how she should feel in response.

"Have a seat," he said.

Hannah apprehensively approached the chair. It was illuminated by a single light that seemed to emanate from out of nowhere. A disembodied light haunting this dark casket. She looked for it. The light certainly wasn't cast down from above her. The void in this room ran completely along the edges, sealing her in here like an insect in a jar.

She sat in the chair.

Mr. Mahogany pasted a few of the sensors to Hannah's shoulders and chest. Immediately the electrocardiograph started beeping faster. She realized her heart was racing. Blood rushed through her veins as if it wanted to stretch its legs one last time before it turned to sap.

"Try to stay calm," said Mr. Mahogany.

He strapped her arms down to the chair's arms and bound her legs to the legs of the chair.

Hannah did not like this. She instinctively struggled against the bindings, but it was no use.

The teacher walked over to the far end of the room and opened what appeared to be a closet in the wall. Inside were strings. Dozens and dozens of strings, bundled up like spaghetti. Some were thin for more nuanced movements, like the ones that would go through ends of her hands and fingers. Others were thick, like the feeding string, which had to be wide enough to allow the puppetfeed to travel down.

Mr. Mahogany wrapped a few of them up in his palm. She heard a squishing sound and looked over. Instead of hands, he too had two slimy slug-like feelers coming out of the ends of his wrist, just like the Jordanpuppet did.

His feet clopped against the tiled floor as he slowly walked back over to her.

"I'm scared," eked Hannah, looking helplessly towards her teacher.

He didn't say anything back. He didn't acknowledge her in the slightest. He rested the pile of strings on her chest as he hit a few buttons and knobs on the machine next to her. Hannah's heart beat at the pace of a horse's gallop. Mr. Mahogany switched the monitor screen off. Aside from the creaky movements of his body, the room went silent.

An electric razor buzzed. But only for a second. A thick lock of her hair fell to the floor. He had shaved a quarter-sized patch on the top of her head.

He then picked up the feeding string. The end of it was metal and it came to a sharp point. It was like a giant hypodermic needle, as thick as a finger. He didn't bother sterilizing it.

Hannah once again struggled futilely against her bindings.

"I don't want this," Hannah whispered to herself. "What am I doing? I do not want this."

As he pulled the feeding string across her face, a globule of puppetfeed leaked out. It fell like a raindrop and landed directly on Hannah's lips before rolling into her mouth and down her throat.

She only had enough time to register the taste. Bitter. Like decaying fruit. Then:

She seized. She went rigid and her eyes sprung open as wide as they could spring. Her whole being shook, not just her body, but the ineffable essence through which she defined the world. Color disappeared. It drained out of everything. She could only see in various shades of black and white; the monochromatic prison of her arrested state.

And then, the scene unfolded in her mind in an instant. It was like having her life flash before her eyes, but in reverse. This was a flash of the immediate future. The exquisite and unfathomable pain of having this lightning rod shoved directly into her brain. The puppetfeed flowing in. The amalgam of thoughts she regarded as what made her 'Hannah' being drowned like ants in an underground colony after a violent tempest. All of her bacteria, her cells, the universe within her purged out through her pores. She'd be covered in pus. Drowning in her former self. And then...she couldn't see past that because there was no past that. That was the end of her. She would be wood.

She was still paralyzed as she desperately forced her eyes over to the teacher looming above her. The water that ran out of her tear ducts wasn't just because of sadness, though the sadness that accompanied them was evident. These tears were also because of frustration. Because of stress. Because of humility. Because of physical strain. Her tears were every kind of tear rolled into one.

Her teacher didn't look at her. He couldn't. His head had flung back on the hinges of his mouth. Two gnarled claws came out of his throat hole. They were covered in woodpulp and wriggling tiny insect larva, smelling like death and rot.

He didn't seem to be in pain though. He continued performing his task. His wooden feet clopped on the tile once more, until he was standing behind her.

Hannah's eyes now rolled up. She looked at the black void. The endless dark black that was deep and eternal and full of nothing, and it was everywhere. Nothingness everywhere.

But then:

She saw that tiny light start to sparkle again. Directly above. Amidst all that black.

And a moment later, a second tiny light appeared.

And then a third. A fourth.

More and more.

For a moment, she forgot where she was and what was about to happen to her. What are these strange lights? she wondered. She was enraptured by the bizarre fireworks display that now seemed to filled up the void. Hundreds of lights. Thousands. Millions. Maybe even more. It seemed to go on endlessly. Twinkling like...like...

Stars.

They were stars.

She had only read of stars in books. She thought they were fiction. Made-up. But there they were like grains of salt spilt all over a picnic blanket. It was the most beautiful thing she had ever seen.

And suddenly Hannah knew she had made a grave mistake in allowing herself to come into this room.

Mr. Mahogany stood above her head, needle in his vulgar hand. She could feel the heat of the creature inside of him and it dripped pulpy mucus on her. She concentrated.

She focused all her energy. She could feel it building in her, rolling like thunder, crashing like clouds, burning like fire. She trembled, opened her mouth, and with everything inside of her she cried out:

HELP!

Twenty-Three

Help.

That was the final and futile word that passed through Hannah's lips, as weak as a droplet of water leaking out of a faucet.

It was no use.

Her appeal had not the legs by which to escape the room. It had not the muscle to even be heard. It was a quiet and desperate plea burped out at a decibel just above a prayer. A pathetic and last-ditch effort to evade the end that was soon to be hers.

And were fortune as benevolent as it was made out to be, Hannah's voice might've been able to find a meager wind on which to ride. Her voice would've been carried out of this chamber on the wings of a fortuitous breeze. It would've floated over the top of the walls. It would've become a cloud itself and rained back down into the hallway. Her plea would've been thunder. And it wouldn't have gotten lost amidst the din like it did. It wouldn't have disappeared into the excited chorus of clucking students, themselves eager to finally graduate into adulthood. Hannah's voice would've found its way, against all logic and against all odds, into Bette's waiting ears.

But there's no such thing as fortune. No such thing as fate.

Every creature, big and small, has and will always be on its own.

So when Bette decided to step out of the line and walk up to the FINAL TESTING ROOM, when she shoved her way past the shocked puppet teacher guarding the door, when she burst into the dark room to save her cousin, it was not luck. Nor was it destiny. It was because she thought of Hannah as one of the strongest and most fiercely individualistic people she had ever known. It's because she admired her cousin. She admired her rebellion, even if she were too afraid to rebel herself. And she realized that her hero, the person she secretly looked up to the most, was about to lose all the things that made her so much *her.* And she didn't want that for Hannah.

And so she acted.

The feeding tube in Mr. Mahogany's crooked tentacle hovered just an inch from the top of Hannah's skull when Bette appeared in the doorway and screamed out:

"STOP!"

Mr. Mahogany looked up. Bette's eyes immediately went wide with fear.

His entire body had split in two, all the way down to his waist. Splintered and slivered wood stuck up from his beltline like barren trees stripped by fire. And coming out of his ruptured torso were spindly white legs. Six of them. They were moist and covered in clear, thornthick spikes. Like the streams of a fountain, the insect sprouted from his puppet waist in long, swooping arches. His head had been destroyed. It was caved in and full of holes like it had long ago rotted away from the inside. Grubby white worms spilled out his empty eye sockets and broken jaw. The larva pooled up on the floor. She could hear the wood continuing to creak. To stress. Whatever was inside of him was pushing out against the trunk of his body; it hadn't fully hatched yet.

"Hannah?" said Bette.

Mr. Mahogany made a guttural hissing sound at her.

"Bette? Is that you?" Hannah gasped. "Oh my god!" she sobbed. "Help me! Please! I'm tied down!"

Before Bette could make a move, the teacher blindly charged at her. Bette leapt to the side and landed on her shoulder on the floor. She winced in pain but managed to scramble over to behind the back of Hannah's chair. She quickly undid her bindings. Hannah was free.

Hannah stood up on the chair as Mr. Mahogany again attempted to tackle her cousin. Bette once again barely escaped.

Mrs. Balsa entered the room. She stood there for a moment. Her silhouette took up the majority of the doorframe.

For a fleeting second she watched the scene unfold before her, but then her body suddenly went rigid as if frozen. As if she was reverting back into a tree. And then her torso split like she had been struck by an axe. Scraggly alien legs clawed their way out of the hole in her body too, grasping violently at the air before turning their attention to the two girls.

A cluster of thick strings dangled in front of Hannah like an unwashed angel's hair. She grabbed a handful, leapt up into the air, and swung, striking Mrs. Balsa in the chest. The teacher went sprawling backwards across the floor, though she was not completely stunned by the blow. As soon as the momentum from the kick stopped, the knotted bug legs were crawling back towards the melee.

"What is happening!?" cried Bette as she once again narrowly dodged Mr. Mahogany's strike.

"They're not wood," said Hannah. "Or, at least, not totally. There's something inside of them. And it's coming out."

"What is it?"

"I don't know."

Mrs. Balsa's legs struck at Hannah like a spider trying to sink its fangs into its prey. Hannah jerked to the side and avoided the hit, but in the process she ended up getting butted by the back of one of Mr. Mahogany's legs. She fell to the ground, her face instantly caked in a starfish of blood. The larva on the ground writhed under her body, slithering towards her head, trying to burrow in her ears.

Mrs. Balsa regained her composure and saw the teenager helplessly spread out on the floor. She walked over to Hannah. No flurry in her step. Hannah was reeling in pain and had nowhere left to go. Like machetes were the ends of her white legs, stabbing the ground.

Mrs. Balsa raised them above her head.

"All you had to do was fall in line. Listen. And obey." the teacher's voice gurgled through a mouth that was no longer there. "We've always known what was best for you. Life is not so complicated. You didn't have to suffer long. You would've made a beautiful log."

And just as Mrs. Balsa was about to sink the sharpened blades into the fragile flesh of the terrified human girl, Bette came charging out of the corner.

"Leave. Her. ALONE!"

She spear-tackled Mrs. Balsa at the waist and they both tumbled down to the tile.

Hannah took the opportunity to spring to her feet.

"Bette! Come on! Now's our chance!" she shouted as she motioned to the open door.

But before Bette could recover, Mr. Mahogany pounced on her cousin too. The end of one of his legs stabbed its way through Bette's shoulder and pinned her to the floor.

"Run!" Bette cried out to Hannah.

"I can't leave you!" Hannah yelled back to her cousin.

"You have to!" she said as another leg went through the meat of her other shoulder.

"But...but...they're going to..."

"I know," said Bette no longer screaming. A look of serenity had come across her face. Mrs. Balsa gathered up the nearby strings and held them over the girl. Bette looked at Hannah and actually smiled. "I worked my ass off my whole life to get to this point. I did everything right. It was my decision. I chose this, Hannah. It's okay. Everything is going to be okay..."

And then Mrs. Balsa plunged the hypodermic end of the feeding tube through the top of Bette's skull.

Immediately, the puppetfeed started flowing into her.

Her eyes rolled up. Up to the firmament. Up to the void.

"Hannah, I can see the stars!" she weakly exclaimed.

And a moment later all of her organs liquefied. All of her bones dissolved. All of her cells died. Everything inside of her foamed up like bath suds and exuded out of her eyes and nose and mouth and ears in a swath of pink froth. Her flesh sizzled as she disappeared into a cloud of her own biology. And when the cloud disappeared, when the bubbles all popped and the slime that used to be Bette was nothing more than a puddle on which the worms fed, there was nothing but a wooden puppet version of her younger cousin left. No fear on her face. No sadness or pain. Just another piece of driftwood cast against the sea of time.

Hannah didn't wait around any longer.

She burst through the FINAL TESTING ROOM door.

She was bruised and dirty and disheveled and covered in blood. The kids in line saw her and fell silent. Like a wave, the attention of the entire student body was pulled forward to the beaten and bedraggled girl now standing in front of them.

"Run!" Hannah shouted to everyone. "It's a trap!"

Twenty-Four

She stood there with wide and wild eyes.

Were the sun available to activate the orange that hid in her irises, it surely would've made them glow like fire. But the void here was vast, dark and deep, and there wasn't enough light to feed them color. Instead, she let her chest heave in and out like she was hemorrhaging air and hoped her flared nostrils were enough to convey her sincerity.

But no one did anything.

Nobody moved.

She was greeted with skepticism. Her classmates stood dumbfounded. It was as if she were committing some sort of heinous social faux pas, as if her words were spilt milk dribbling out of her mouth.

Befuddled students regarded her with an abject bemusement. Puzzled stares. Some even snickered, like it was all just a joke. Perhaps, had they just a few moments more, the student body's collective scorn would've segued into full-blown mockery, but no sooner had Hannah said those words did Mr. Mahogany and Mrs. Balsa burst out of the room behind her. Their horrifying, disfigured frames cracked and split and erupting with insect flesh.

Then it was pandemonium.

Then it was chaos.

Then the other kids listened.

But it was too late.

Hannah shoved her way through the panicked crowd. Bodies flowed around her like liquid through a channel and she disappeared into the bristling mass. Just another raindrop in this river of hysteria.

The students who tripped were gracelessly trampled. Their weak and malleable anatomies squished beneath the heft of the stampede. Hannah tried to step around them, but she couldn't. She had no other direction to go, lest she end up on the floor too. She plodded through the slop of her fallen friends. The dead bodies not acting as a bridge to cross, but rather a swamp she was forced to wade through.

From other classrooms more teachers emerged. It was like an alarm had sounded and all the sentries had been released at once.

At first they moved like manikins, rigid and mechanical, but soon their stiff limbs broke off. Snapped away like twigs, and in their place were crispy white insect legs, wildly grasping at the air. Bodies ruptured and cracked, revealing the fetid exoskeletal crust underneath. Heads split open, white jaws chewing through the wood from the inside, spewing forth a rancid font of vomit, mealworms, maggots, and grubs.

More students around her were felled to the monsters hatching from out of the adults. But as violent as their methods were, they were not killing the children they caught. Any death was brought on accidently by fellow human hands as they desperately scrambled to get away. Instead, the insects would wrap their segmented limbs around their prey and quickly plunge a feeding tube into the tops of their skulls. Before a protest could even be uttered, before the pain could be registered and internalized, the puppetfeed flowed. The transformation occurred. Just like that.

And Hannah realized this wasn't a massacre. It was a mass conversion.

Strings were stabbed through hands and feet and knotted on the other end. So sharp were the needled ends of these strings that they passed through bone as if it were nothing more than butter. Purged organs and now-useless blood made up the slick pink foam that covered the floor as the grubs and worms writhed their way into the gaping faces of the now metamorphosed students.

They trembled, convulsed, and then rose themselves. Wood.

Adulthood complete.

Hannah sloshed through the muck, unsure of what to do, what was happening, where to go.

She eventually found an empty classroom and closed and locked the door behind her. Still, through the walls, she could hear her classmates scream. She could hear the clamor. The struggle. The inevitable defeat. The wet squish of the world gone mad.

She pushed her back up against door and cried.

And one by one, into the void above, she could see the puppets get yanked up into oblivion. Just like Dr. Alder did back in his office. They disappeared into the stars.

The stars.

What were the stars?

Where did they come from?

Had they always been there, hidden from her, or were they brand new?

The clamor outside the room slowly subsided. From each throat, the final scream had been wrought. All the humanity had been purged. All the monsters, uprooted and erased in the great big black sky.

She was alone.

Except for the single knock on the other side of the door.

She quickly scooted across the floor and tried not to make any noise and tried not to breathe and she used her hands to stifle her sobs and she used a desk to shield herself from whatever horror had just arrived.

But then came a voice. A familiar voice. A voice she knew almost as intimately as her own, except as it spoke through the paper thin walls, it carried none of the condescending and judgmental tone with which Hannah defined as its hallmark. This version of the voice was soft. Full of love and sympathy.

"Hannah, it's Mom," her mompet said. "Please open the door and let me in."

Twenty-Five

"Mom?"

"Honey, are you okay?" her mother said "What are you doing in there? Stop messing around and let me in."

"No."

"What do you mean 'no'?"

"You're one of them, aren't you?"

"One of who?"

"One of them!" Hannah cried out. "One of the monsters!"

"Monsters?" her confused mother said. "C'mon, Hannah. Stop being silly. You know there are no such thing as monsters."

"They're inside of you," said Hannah. "I've seen them. They feed on your wood."

Her mompet paused and let silence fill up the empty space. It was a silence so swollen it was as if her mother had left and in her place stood a hole so wide no sound could ever cross it. In this silence, Hannah disappeared. The world disappeared. But then, when her mother eventually did respond, the words hit Hannah with the full force of gravity.

"They're inside of you, too, darling."

And in that instant, there was only fear. Hannah felt as if her spine were a bear trap, or her body were a prison. Everything inside of her went tight. Even her ribcage seemed to shrink. *They're inside of you, too.* Like the wind in the darkness, a whirr seemed to strip the words of all meaning until they too became white noise, an inexorable drone, a new kind of silence even uglier than before.

Slowly Hannah climbed to her feet. She walked over to the classroom door and apprehensively flipped the lock. The click of the latch disengaging echoed down the hall. Hannah retreated back a few steps as the door swung open like the yawning jaw of a marionette.

Her mother stood there, centered in the doorframe like a model in a painting. Like a doll in a box on the shelf at the store.

The school behind her had been eerily returned to normal. Any trace of the carnage that had been there minutes ago was now gone. There were no maniacal teachers with their split-alien trunks, no untenable students begging for their fragile lives, no more puddles of expunged human viscera coating the walls and floors like a hurricane of blood had just blown through.

Her mother was alone and the school looked as it always had.

Her mother held out her arms. Opened wide, like she wanted a hug. For a moment Hannah held back. Her mother wanted a hug? She knew this was a trap. Of course it was a trap. It HAD to be a trap. But Hannah was not granite. And she was not wood. She was a human being with human emotions that were more varied and colorful than the smear of a rainbow.

The levee of her composure slowly cracked and she found herself running to return her mother's embrace.

"Mommy," Hannah cried out.

Tears ran down the contours of her nose, leaving their salty trail across her lips. Like battery acid this sorrow felt. And she thought as a puppet not only would she not be able to cry anymore, but she wouldn't be able to taste the vinegar tang of her own sadness. She could be free of all of this. These moments of helplessness, this existential pain that seemed to taint even her happiest memories.

"I don't know what's happening to me," she wept into her mother's cedar chest.

"It's all perfectly natural," her mother said. "Just a part of growing up..."

From the space underneath her mompet's eyes and along the hinges of her mouth, a moistness had started to form. Almost as if her mother were trying to shed a tear too.

"The less you fight the easier it will be," her mompet said. "I love you, Hannah. We all do. We only want what is best for you."

Her eyes fell out of her head; rolled across the floor like billiard's balls. She kept hugging her daughter though -not tight, but tender- as her jaw slid off like it were made of melted ice cream.

Hannah gulped. Pushed her way out of the hug and backed up a step. She stood up straight and looked at this decaying thing in front of her that she once called her mother.

"What are you?" she said with equal parts shock and horror.

"There's only one world, Hannah," her mompet's voice gurgled out of the throat hole on her mouthless face. "One life you're given. One chance to live it. There's no escaping that. Unless you let me give you a way," she said as she motioned to her strings.

"You have to understand that there are things more horrible than you could imagine pumping through your veins. Do you want your body to just be a shantytown for an untold number of bacteria and diseases? *They* are the real monsters, Hannah. They don't care about you. They will poison you and slowly eat away at you. They are using you up and they will leave you for dead. You are their incubator. You are their lunch."

Her mompet's hair now fell out. Already matted and congealed with pulpy mucus, when it hit the floor it made a plop. Hannah breathed deep, her body electric and tense, full of so much adrenaline it was almost too much for her to bear. It was as if her insides were trying to escape. Like her skeleton were passing through her like a cruise ship through an ocean.

"...Of course, we will all be eaten away by time. It's a sad inevitability that we all must face," her mother continued. She motioned up to the black void above. "The void awaits us all. And there's no cure for that. Even when you turn to wood, they can repair, resand, repaint, but eventually the mulch is where we all must lay. We can't take that fate away, but what we can do is offer you a life without complication. Without angst. Without fear or dread. It only hurts a little bit," she said. "And then it never hurts again..."

And as she said that, her face completely fell away. It just dropped off like a pine tree would drop a cone. And underneath the wooden mask that made up the familiar figure Hannah knew as Mom, there was the face of an insect. A termite, to be exact. White and blind. Covered in slime and hair-thin flagella. Antenna vibrating like a tuning fork. Two thick pincers made up the creature's mouth, snapping reflexively with the cadence of her breath. Her mompet's hands then broke off, too, and out of the tips of her arms came fleshy claws.

"You're a termite?!" Hannah shrieked.

"It's okay, babygirl," her mother cooed through her twisted insect grin. "The Puppeteer takes care of us. When we start to rot, he yanks us up and replaces our broken parts and returns us to the ground as good as new. And then the cycle starts again. This isn't an infestation. It's an understanding, a balance, a *dance*, you could say. You did want to dance, didn't you Hannah? This is life. There's no reason to be afraid of me. To be afraid of the future. All you have to do is stop fighting and grow up..."

Her mother held up the feeding string.

"Grow up and give in."

Hannah's eyes went from the sharpened end of the crusted syringe back to her mother's gnarled termite face. Hannah was exhausted. Tired of running. Tired of fighting. And her mother, although an insect inside, now radiated outward with this alien sort of affection to such an extreme, Hannah could barely recognize her at all. It was as if she saw her mother for the first time as an entity outside of what she did for her. And yet, in that instant, it wasn't liberation that she felt. It was more like reflection, full of remorse. She wanted nothing more than to be cradled in her mother's insect legs. She wanted to apologize for everything she had ever done, but she knew that her mompet had already forgiven her and it was all a mountain of useless yesterdays cluttering up the back of her mind. Now all she wanted to do was make her termite-mother happy.

Puppetfeed flowed down the string, ready to be injected into Hannah's brain. As gray and as thick as oatmeal. Hannah walked towards her long-suffering mompet, but just before accepting her embrace and the embrace of the needle itself, she stopped. There was only one question left to ask, and Hannah couldn't allow herself to take another step forward without at least saying it.

"But what about the stars, mama?"

"What stars?" the insect said.

"Up in the void. The stars that showed up and twinkled. It's not all darkness. What about the stars?"

Her mother looked up at the sky and then back down to daughter.

"There's no stars in the void," she said.

But there were. Hannah looked up too and she could see them. So many stars. Endless amounts. A star for every bacteria that made up her body. A star for every wish that could possibly be conceived.

Hannah froze.

"Honey?" said her mother.

"I'm sorry," was Hannah's raspy reply.

"What?"

"I'm not going with you."

"What do you mean you're not coming with me?" her confused mother said.

"I can't."

Her mompet stood there a moment, considering what she had just been told. And then she leapt onto her daughter. She pinned her to the ground with her pointed claws. She lowered her face so it was just inches above Hannah's. Wide segmented eyes regarded her with fury.

"I love you, Hannah!" the termite gurgled through its wet mandible. "Why do you hurt me? I can't allow you to keep suffering as this bag of flesh when such a glorious future surely awaits you. You have to grow up. You HAVE to! I only want what's best for you. Best for you. Best for you. Best for you. Best for you. Best for you. Best for you. Best for you. Best for you. Best for you. Best for you. Best for. Best for. Best for. Best for. Best for. Best for. Best. Best. Best. Best. Best. Best. Best. Bes-Bes-Bes-Be-Be-Be-Be-B-B-B-B-B"

Hannah spun around and started to feebly crawl her way across the floor, although she knew it was useless. Her mother was spry. Her mother was immune to pain. Her mother moved with the litheness of a mosquito and quickly shuffled over to her fleeing daughter to hold her to the floor under her splintered foot.

"Just know, Hannah, that I'll love you forever, despite all the grief you've caused me."

And then she stabbed the feeding tube into the back of Hannah's head.

The puppetfeed hit her brain like the crack of thunder. If this feeling had fingers it would've been squeezing her from the inside. Had it a voice it would've been screaming throughout her every cell. A rigidity collected up in her joints as the wood process began to take hold. She could feel herself fading away and this doppelganger coming up from the darkness to take her place. She was disappearing into herself. She had to stop it. She had to do something. She had to try.

She swung her arms around and tried pulling the string out of her head, but tiny barbs at the end caught on the inside of her skull and kept it from sliding back out the way it came. Her fingernails slid off in a flurry of expelled meat. Her pores started to ooze pink. She grit her teeth and fell to her knees. There was only one other option left, the only hope she ultimately had, and the prospect of it was so terrifying that had she given it a second's more thought, she wouldn't have been able to even attempt it.

She pushed the feeding string in deeper.

It sliced through the sponge of her teenage brain, severing untold numbers of neural connections. She felt pieces of her personality break off like ice drifts. More feed filled up those empty spaces. But still deeper she pushed. Deeper. Until she could no longer bear it. Until she flickered in and out of existence. Until her memory of anything else faded and pain was the only sensation that ever was.

Her limbs went stiff.

Splinters rose from her skin like hair.

She fell to her knees and with her last bit of strength she pushed the string in even deeper because deeper was the only way she could go. And just as she were about to resign and give her half-wooden casket of a body to the gully graveyard where all failed puppets end, the needle tip of the feeding string erupted out the other side of her head.

The pain instantly stopped. As did the wood conversion process. The puppetfeed slowly ceased pumping. Hannah's eyes were bloodshot and wide but they were still intact and the end of the feeding string stuck straight out from the center of her forehead. And as she climbed back onto her feet, she caught a quick glimpse at her reflection in her mother's alien, mucus-covered face.

The metal rod looked like a unicorn's horn.

And then Hannah gripped the end of the feeding string in both her hands and pulled. The needle passed completely through her head, the tube arching in a loop around her like she had just been sewn into the sky. She held it in her hand like a harpoon.

"You didn't want what was best for me," Hannah said to her termite-mother. "You have no idea what's best for me. You only wanted to make me more like you because that's what you know, what you were comfortable with, when the truth is, you and I are not even the same species."

"Hannah..."

"They say puppets can't feel fear," Hannah continued. "But I don't think that's true. I think that puppets feel more fear than anyone. They push it down, try to ignore it, try their hardest to pretend it's not there. But it is there. It's everywhere. It exists in everyone and everything. And if you don't acknowledge it, it'll gnaw away at you from the inside. Eat you up. Turn you into something you never wanted to be in the first place. But not me, mother. I refuse to ignore it. I will not bury it away and let it corrupt me like a weed growing in the back of the garden. I'd rather feel miserable than feel nothing at all. So I will *become* the fear. I will HURT and SUFFER. And I will never stop fighting."

And with that, she plunged the end of feeding tube into her mother's oakbarrel chest.

It stuck in the wood like an arrow. Without hesitation, Hannah stepped up onto it. Then onto her mother's head. The termite hissed and bit at her legs, but Hannah ignored her. She leapt off her mother and wrapped her fingers around the string that was stitched through her forehead.

And she began to climb.

"Hannah, what are you doing? Come back here!" the insect called from the ground. "You can't do this, Hannah! You can't go up there! You have to stop!"

But Hannah didn't stop.

She climbed out of the roof of the school and up over the entire town and she could look out and see the whole world lain out flat like a dinner plate. The Suburbs and The City, side-by-side like sisters at a cotillion, separated only by the graveyard of dead puppets that bisected the planet like the two hemispheres of a brain.

Beyond that, there was nothing. No other towns or cities. No oceans or forests. The world was flat, and it dropped off into an even larger void that surrounded and swallowed up everything outside of the dim light of this puppet stage.

Higher still she climbed.

Up past the clouds.

Past the sky itself.

She climbed until she left this world completely.

She climbed until she entered the void.

Twenty-Six

Hannah's brow was moist with sweat and her heart beat at a hummingbird's pace and her stomach churned like a stone in a mill and her nostrils flared and the flesh from the center of her hands was ruptured and ripped and all she wanted to do was go to sleep, but fist after fist she continued her ascension, leaving chunks of her palms stuck to the outside of the feeding tube like her skin were made of glue. Hot gore ran down the claret-stained string, globs of meat like chum on a fishing line, disappearing into the everlasting night that now settled around her.

Up here she was alone. More alone than she had ever been. More alone than anyone in history had ever been. A new level of loneliness that was impenetrable by even her thoughts, her thoughts torn asunder as the string continued to pass through the hole in her head, her thoughts all scrambled up like the picture on an old television set. All she could do was struggle to exist. There was silence in which not even a *woosh* of air came by to fill. She was in a vacuum. She was in outer space.

The school was completely out of sight. As was the town. The world became smaller and smaller. A few miles up and the entire planet looked as small as a saucer. A few miles more and it seemed the size of a penny. The people and puppets on it got smaller too, shrinking down, each person no bigger than a grain of sand. A world of sand.

And then it was gone.

She was tired. Beaten. Cold. But even in her moribund and twilit state, the darkness dared not steal everything completely away and she could still see, at distances unfathomably far from where she dangled, that the stars still twinkled like the lamplights of distant armies. And there were still strings spanning the cosmos around her.

She knew these strings were tethered to a terminus that was way beyond the breadth of her sight – the hands and heads and hastily carved hearts of the puppet people on the bug-infested planet she had just escaped – but she didn't know what lay at the other end towards which she was climbing. Now the universe looked like it were a harp. An exquisite instrument she didn't understand and couldn't play.

Hand over hand. Fist by fist.

Wispy fibers crisscrossed each other like spider-spun webs. And the higher she climbed the tighter the strings were drawn. So thick not even a compass would have been able to point her to true north.

Still she climbed, undaunted, yet fatigue was sinking its razor claws into her muscles. Her frail human muscles. Her fallible human body. So tiny. So weak.

And then it slowly came into view like the flash from a lighthouse. Like a candle over black waters. Like the chirp of a torpedo suddenly singing out across a radar screen.

The moon.

All the strings were leading straight up to the moon.

Hannah's mouth hung open in awe. It was so big and so *REAL* and had she anyone around her to share this moment, the words she would've shared would've failed them both anyway.

She was overwhelmed. It was the most beautiful thing she had ever seen.

And then the exhaustion won.

And she let go.

And she fell.

She plummeted through the darkness as if there were still a concept of up and down. As if gravity still had a reason to assert itself. Because from this vantage point, there was no ground for her to even fall back on. She let go and she was lost in oblivion. She fell and would keep falling, forever.

But it didn't happen quite like that.

She didn't disappear because the string that had passed through the center of her forehead suddenly went taut. Her unconscious body caught with a jerk. She bobbed a bit, then went still. And for a moment she sat there swinging like the pendulum of a great grandfather clock before she started to get reeled back up.

Slowly. Delicately. Something was dragging her somnolent frame upward.

Through the maze of strings she passed, through the gossamer membrane of wire and twine that separated the void and the sky. Though the nothingness of the universe eternal.

It pulled her up.

And dropped her off on the surface of the moon.

Twenty-Seven

The void of unconsciousness was blacker and wider than the void of space, and when the darkness of her mind was suddenly inverted it collapsed in on itself like a dying star. And it was from this place of abject nothingness that Hannah's eyes slowly opened and reality haphazardly pieced itself back together.

She wasn't sure how long she had been out for. It didn't really matter anyway. Up here, time had lost all meaning. There was only this moment, the NOW, the interminably long RIGHT NOW as it stretched like an over-wrought rubber band being pulled in every direction at once.

The feeding tube had been removed from her forehead. Now there was only a swollen hole that went completely through the back of her brain and out the front side. Pink, threadbare veins spread across her face like a veil, like the network of strings in which she had just been lost.

She laid in a bed of fine, powdery dust. She breathed it in until it felt like her insides were full of concrete. She coughed until her eyes watered. There was no color up here. Just different shades of gray; white as it worked its way back to black.

Slowly, she found the strength to climb to her feet. She looked around. Craters rose up around her like tar-stained lungs. But this world was dead. The mountains dared not to breathe. The wind dared not to blow.

She began to walk. Past the Sea of Tranquility and the Ocean of Storms. Past the Lake of Death and the Lake of Sorrow. Distance became as irrelevant as time. Having no way to calculate the how long it took to get from one place to another, a mile might as well have been a foot and a foot might as well have lasted a mile.

But eventually the path in front of her began to grow smaller and it was clear to her this was the way she was supposed to go, and that she was headed in the direction of *something*.

The rocks that lined her trail were tall. And with each passing step she took, they started to morph. Change shape. Take on a more human-esque appearance. Their rounded shoulders and knobby heads, shoulder to shoulder like a hall of sarcophagi. No faces or features, no fingers or toes. Just stone sentinels standing at attention, as if they were terracotta warriors guarding an ancient temple.

Without so much as a nod, a blink, a movement of any sort, they led her down this quickly narrowing road. She apprehensively stepped, mile after mile, foot after foot.

And then, at the end of this path, she came upon a great mountain that rose up taller than even the tallest skyscrapers that purveyed The City. But this mountain seemed odd. It did not come to a sharp peak at the top like the kind of mountains you'd find in a geography book. Nor did it have any rocks nor crags nor jagged edges to jacket its arching bluffs. It was smooth at the top and bowed out on the sides, as if it were shaped and shorn by a very careful hand.

And as she got even closer, she realized this mountain seemed to quiver. Shake. It was undulating as if it were alive itself. And then it hit her. This wasn't a mountain she was staring at all, but rather, a gigantic hunched over man, his back facing her as he worked on something just out of eyesight.

She apprehensively walked around the base of this man, trying her hardest to overpower the fear that she rightly felt.

At first she was greeted by a forest. Thick and lush and full of trees. It stretched out like a verdant carpet across the surface of the moon, all the way to the far end of the horizon.

She didn't even know the moon could support vegetation, let alone a forest as dense as this.

A massive arm reached out from the mountain and yanked a tree up from the ground. The other hand held a large metal blade with which it began to carve. From this tree he fashioned arms and legs, bendable joints, a head that rocked and a jaw that moved.

And next to this giant mountain man was a machine. It hummed and whirred and vibrated like a robot reciting poetry. There was no electricity on the moon and Hannah couldn't figure out what was powering the device, though it was clear to her what its purpose was.

It was a loom.

A massive loom.

And it was threading together the strings that sewed up the void and stretched from here back down to her hometown. Occasionally these hands would stop whittling long enough to unhinge a few strings from the machine and attach them to the small wooden figure he had just sculpted, and Hannah knew at once who it was she was beholding, though she could hardly believe it was true.

This was him. This was The Puppeteer.

He sat in the dust, bent over, enthralled in his work. A human, he was, in every form except one. His head. His head was a log. Scaly bark covered his face like a peeling sunburn. His mouth was awkwardly cut, as if notched by an axe, and his nose was like a knot on a picnic table. He was unfinished. Uncarved. In fact, the only human vestige that seemed to defy his oak-wooden face were his eyes. He had soft eyes; dark brown circles that were wide and tired, and his pupils floated in the placid warm white of his sclera, like satellites. There was soul in those eyes as they turned to look at her, and with trembling lips that had grown stiff from disuse this mountain of a man said in a voice like a bulldozer:

"Hannah? Is that you?"

Twenty-Eight

The Puppeteer laid the incomplete puppet body in the dust and bent his vast and alpine frame so that he faced the awestruck child.

"I – I didn't think you were real," was all Hannah could manage.

A congenial smirk like a vine of ivy crept its way across his timber cheeks.

"I didn't think YOU were real, either," he said.

Hannah's fear was eclipsed by a queer and mordant sort of curiosity. Were this mountain going to flatten her, there would be nothing she could do to stop him, but she had the feeling that wasn't something to be concerned about anyway.

"You didn't think I was real?" she said. "What do you mean? Didn't you create me?"

The Puppeteer chuckled.

"No. No, dear. I don't create people. I replace them..." He motioned to the inert, half-whittled doll he had just laid down. "When it comes time for people to step out of their skin, I give them the new skin to climb into..." He then motioned to the mechanical loom that the strings were being woven in. "And then I do my best to make sure no harm comes their way."

Hannah's gaze drifted to the forest growing on the moon. The different trees bundled up like a bouquet of flowers. She knew that one of these trees would've been the one to replace her, had she completed the graduation process. In a way, she was face-to-face with her future self. Unpolished. Unloved. The wood she was about to become.

"Why?" she said.

"Why what?" the giant man responded.

"Why are you up here? Why are you doing this, turning us into puppets? What is the purpose of any of it?"

"Am I being accused of something?" he said. "I could ask that very same questions of you, Hannah. Why are you up here? Why don't you allow yourself to *become* a puppet? What is the purpose of you?"

"I – I don't know," she stammered. "I just...ran. I was trapped. And they were closing in. And I didn't know what else to do and so I climbed."

He sighed.

"You know, I am not a very good puppeteer. I try, but trying never feels like enough. I just wanted to do something meaningful with my life. To matter, in some weird way. We're not that different, you and I. Like you, I too ran, until my options ran out. And like you, I ended up here. An alien entity on an alien planet. A continent of one."

"I just want to know what's wrong with me," she sniffled. "Why can't I be happy? Why must I see the stars when no one else can? Why am I the only one who must answer to the monsters that hide inside everyone else around me?"

"I didn't build your world, Hannah," the Puppeteer mournfully replied. "If I had, I would've taken more care. I would've spent thousands of years crafting every angle, every detail, every nuance. I would've done it right. But I don't have that ability. I cannot create the universe. Instead, I found it. I found you. You were there, on that tiny dusty button you call a planet, just floating in space. And the people there were sad. I found a sad planet. I tried to fix that. I tried to give them purpose. When they were old enough and their bodies were strong, I remade them into wood so they wouldn't have to hurt anymore. I wanted to help them.

"But there were other creatures that lived on the Earth. Things uglier than even the ugliest thing you've ever felt. And in my haste to prove to you all that I could be a worthy and beneficent entity, that I alone could soothe all your existential woes, I hadn't taken these things into account. The planet was full of insects. Under the dirt. Termites. Hungry for wood. They cast up vines from beneath the ground, their own version of strings, and they'd lay their eggs in puppets like incubators waiting for them to hatch. They kept destroying everything I built. Eating away at everything that was decent and good. I had no choice. I had to try and do something to stop them, and *fast*...

"So I dug a gully the length of the entire planet. Like a river of emptiness, between The Suburbs and The City. I cast all the termites into that ditch, forced them into a hole where they couldn't hurt anyone. And I put up a fence to stop people from entering the termite's den.

"But my puppets were sometimes willful. They were sometimes brash. They were sometimes angry that they had to become puppets in the first place. You can understand that, can't you? Every puppet was born a human, after all, and humans are a patchwork of conflicting and complex emotions. Some didn't want their strings. They refused to comply. They resented me and all I had done for them. And so they tried to cross the gully. To escape the comfortable corner of the universe I had whittled for them. And as they tried to make their way to The City, the termites were able to take control. They became infected. And that infection spread its dirty claws over all that I had done, so much so that people didn't even know where this sickness came from. They just knew that it was there, that little voice deep down, scratching away at you from the insides, convincing you to self-destruct.

"Now all I can do is yank up those who are poisoned mad by their termite souls and replace them with a new wooden body. Uninfected. Unaware. Unafraid. I've tried to be scrupulous. I've tried to keep up. But I can't control what happens off the strings. I can't control you, Hannah."

By now, Hannah's cheeks were stained by tears, salt water rivers running through the chalky lunar soot that had settled on her face.

"But, I don't understand. What – what does all this mean?" she blubbered.

"It means, in the basest sense, that you and I are equals, Hannah. In fact..." he trailed of as he motioned above him. There was a void sitting there, much like the ones that floated in the sky above Earth. And coming out of void, directly into to The Puppeteer's back, were strings. They were almost invisible, but they were still there. The Puppeteer himself was attached to strings. "...you might even have a few advantages over me."

Hannah wiped her eyes and looked perplexedly at The Puppeteer's strings.

"Where do those go?"

"I don't know," he shook his head. "I've never been brave enough to find out. The illusion of control is a powerful thing. And so I do as I was meant to do."

"Everything is so complicated. All I wanted to do was dance," Hannah breathlessly said to herself, her worn-out face only able to pull up a blank look. "I didn't want all of this..."

The Puppeteer looked at this sad girl and his heart broke in his colossal chest. So slowly, he swung his legs out from underneath him. Like an earthquake his bones popped, his body almost petrified from remaining still for so long. But through a drumroll of creaks and cracks he moved his limbs, until he was standing next to Hannah, a half-mile tall.

He reached over and plucked one of the strings coming off the loom. A note rung out. A C-sharp. It vibrated across the cosmos, a sound born and expressed in a singular motion.

A smile bit the side of Hannah's mouth, though she tried to stifle it. But The Puppeteer saw this and he plucked a few more strings. *Bing-bing-bing.* Then he began strumming, like a guitar. Music filled up every inch of empty space. Music filled the void. It surrounded Hannah's head and entered her ears and filled up her body like the air itself. And she looked down to see her foot, tapping against her will, as if it usurped every other instinct and was held prisoner by the music.

The giant bent over and held out his massive hand. Without apprehension, Hannah took it. He nodded at her. She nodded back. And the two of them began to dance together.

"This universe we inhabit is our collective burden," he said, slowly turning the swaying girl. "But it is held up by many hands. Even then, there are still burdens not even the universe can bear, and that is the universe that you create..."

He plucked a green apple from one of the trees in the forest and held it out for Hannah. She took it. On one side of the apple the skin was crispy and fresh and looked delicious, but on the other side the skin had rotted off and the white pulp inside had turned moldy and brown. She thought of the bacteria inside of her guts. She was responsible for all of them. Without her, they wouldn't exist either.

"I'm afraid," she said, looking up to the man.

"You can't grow up without letting a little part of yourself go," The Puppeteer said. "We've all got to grow up, Hannah. There's no way to avoid it. The only question left is, how?"

And so she took a bite of the decayed side of apple.

She swallowed its putrid juice and let the spoiled fruit work its way down her esophagus. The sickness she fed was her sickness alone, and acknowledging that did not derail her thoughts any more than ignoring it. Sometimes the sickness felt more like the cure. The music continued to play and the two of them continued to move to it, together.

"Ya know, someone had to invent dancing," he said as he sashayed his massive body across the face of the moon. "Someone had to be the first person in history to dance, right? I always wondered how that happened. Maybe some music was playing. Or maybe it even predated the discovery of music. Maybe it was just the metronomic trickle of a nearby brook as it passed over the felled branches and lilies and stalks of reed. All of a sudden, this guy was inspired. His head started bobbing. His feet started tapping. And instead of wondering why all this was happening, he just went with it. Surely, it must've felt like madness. He stood up and he danced while everyone else sat perfectly still around him and thought 'What the hell is wrong with you?'"

The song stopped and the music tapered off. Faded out. Disappeared.

"I can't stay here," Hannah solemnly said.

"I know," he replied. "This is my planet. I wouldn't let you even if you tried."

"Can you tell me where I'm supposed to go now though?" she asked him.

"Well now, that's not my place. You're going to have to tell me."

Hannah thought about it for a moment. And before she could even respond The Puppeteer nodded as if he already knew.

Silently, he fastened a big loop out of a spare string. Hannah sat on it like it were a tire swing. He stepped up to the edge of the moon and held her over the schism of space. Her feet dangled in the void.

Below, ever-faintly, she could see the Earth twinkling, almost imperceptibly, until it was as indistinguishable as the stars in the sky.

"Will I ever see you again?" she asked him.

He shook his head.

"No."

And then he lowered her.

Twenty-Nine

It was a long time before she touched back down on the ground.

She sat like a diamond in a necklace as the teardrop-shaped loop slid its way across these wide, celestial gills.

The Puppeteer returned her back to the Earth. But he did not place her down in The Suburbs. She did not return to her house, her street, her school, her town. She had no desire to go back there. For her, home was no longer a tangible place, but rather, an abstract concept, a foreign nation, a fever-dream lingering in the outskirts of her mind.

By then the Puppeteer had gotten the termite infestation under control. At least temporarily. The struggle between the soil and sky was an eternal one. Insects still burrowed beneath the dirt, sending vines reaching up for new skeletons to infect, worming their way into all those empty wooden puppet chests, the cavities left in the places where their hearts once thumped.

Her mompet and dadpet's defective and splintered bodies had been replaced with fresh new ones, their rosy smiles repainted as forced and as blithe as they've ever been. Perhaps they had no recollection of the parasites that had been hibernating inside of them. Or maybe they did. Maybe they remembered every painful detail. Maybe becoming wood made things like that okay. But, to Hannah, it didn't matter much either way. Not anymore. Her body was not there to play host to the vermin. She was a work of a different kind of art, a temple not crafted by some reckless god's incompetent hands. Her place in this world had yet to be carved.

She touched down in the center of The City. The loop

retracted back into the sky. No strings hung for her. She was free.

But after taking a look around, she quickly realized The City was not exactly what she thought it would be.

The buildings here were not really buildings. She wasn't able to tell from the distance of The Suburbs, but up close she could see that the skyscrapers were just cardboard cutouts with the façades of buildings hastily drawn on them in magic marker. Similarly, traffic lights were made out of plastic and painted to look real, mailboxes didn't open, fire hydrants contained no water, manholes led to nowhere.

This was a fake city. A facsimile. She was standing in a giant dioramic model.

But even more than that, as she walked slowly up and down the avenues of this ghost town, she called out:

"Hello?"

To which she got no response.

She was alone. Completely alone.

There was not another human to be seen. No footprints for her to follow. This cardboard city wasn't just deserted; it had never even been lived in. And then it struck her, a revelation so stark and heavy that it might as well be the onus of all creation.

No one had ever made it this far. No one had ever crossed the gully. She was the only one. It was only her.

And heartbreakingly, because of this, there was nothing substantial or exciting here to save her. Nothing to bolster her. Nothing to make her somebody or something different than what she had always been. She came to The City expecting relief, a grand understanding, *something*, but instead she had gotten a mirror without a reflection. A blank page. This place wasn't constructed to save her. It wasn't built with Hannah in mind. It was just there, like a rock or a tree or the moon itself, forever hidden behind a void.

She wandered around, without aim, without purpose.

She spent long periods lost. Feeling sad. Mourning herself. She spent even longer periods feeling nothing at all. She was a little girl again, a tiny acorn, trapped in a system much bigger and colder than she could imagine. Loneliness held her prisoner and never let her go. Solitude: this was the ultimate price she had to pay for freedom.

She walked until she no longer felt like walking. Until she had nowhere left to go. She sat down in the middle of the street, and there she stayed, like a statue herself. She didn't move. Didn't do anything. And time set moss to grow upon her back. Her bones grew still and stiff and petrified. And still she remained, an unbloomed seed planted on barren land.

And then, an indeterminately long time after that, a thought came to her from seemingly out of nowhere. Because some thoughts are like that. Some thoughts take years, decades, eternities to come together. And then, like the sun rising on the distant horizon, this thought stretched its golden tentacles across her brain, illuminating a singular and simple idea that before had been shrouded by her own sorrow and self-doubt.

And she began to dig.

It took a long time to get through the concrete because she had no tools to aid her besides her hands. She endured broken nails and bloody fingers as she clawed at the pavement like a rodent trapped in an aqueduct. But time fells everything, and eventually she was able to get past the stone that separated her from the soil underneath. She then dug into the ground, pulling out handfuls of cool dirt, leaving them in piles all around her. Termite grubs wiggled around in the mud, but she ignored them. They couldn't hurt her. Not anymore.

When she was done, the hole in front of her was several feet wide and several feet deep. An empty ditch, full of air and nothing else. But only for a brief moment.

No sooner had she finished digging did she take up a pinch of displaced dirt and compact it so it all clumped together. She worked carefully, methodically. She molded the earth into a shape she was intimately familiar with. A head, two arms, two legs, a torso.

It was a little person designed in her own image. A little person to call her own.

But that wasn't all. She then did it again.

And again.

And again.

And again, until there were millions of people lined up in front of her. An entire race of them. Yet they were still just balls of dirt. Static. Cold. Dead. She wanted them to move, to be alive, to do something, anything, but she didn't know how. But no sooner had she huffed in frustration did it occur to her that she had been carrying the solution to this problem with her for her entire life.

One by one, she spit on each muddy little person's head. The bacteria from her body, the bacteria that she had loved and harbored inside her belly like it was her own child was present in that spit. Countless numbers of tiny bacteria teemed in every drop of saliva, every dollop of mucus. She was almost overflowing with it. She was a giant incubator, full of microbes and germs and diseases. And she had so much to share.

The spit soaked its way into the tiny man's frame. Infected his mud body.

And then, slowly, he began to twitch awake.

He was alive.

She scooped him up and lowered him gently into the hole.

She repeated this process. A million times she repeated this process. She did this until she animated the entire population of creatures she had created. She took the universe from inside of her and put it into a hole in the ground.

But the act of creation was simply not enough. She wanted her world to be different than the one she knew, the one she grew up in, the one that had never been kind to people like her.

So she didn't pull hairs out of her head and twist them up into braids and tether up the hands and feet of her people. She didn't want to control them. She was not going to be a puppeteer. She was a human being, and she wanted to give them human things. And so she plunged her hands into her own chest. Her sternum was softer than the concrete street and her fingers sunk through her bone without much effort. She pulled apart her ribcage like a bird spreading its wings, and yanked out her heart in one clean motion. Veins snapped, blood sprayed like a fountain from her now-empty torso. She held the organ in her hand. It pumped. *Lub-dub, lub-dub.* This thing had been her metronome, her lighthouse, her only compass for so long.

And now she was giving it to them.

She placed her heart in the center of the hole. And it continued to beat. Continued to pump. And although it lay there as plain as day for all her people to see - a symbol of her undying and ultimate devotion - it did not bless those around it with the kind of unconditional understanding she had hoped it would. Unfortunately, hearts aren't built that way. The world isn't built that way.

Her people went about their normal lives without any expectation or convention, unaware that such a sacrifice had been made for them. That she had to expunge her own humanity in order for them to fully evolve. In the hole she had dug, each moment of happiness was reciprocated by a moment of sadness. Each feeling of joy was buoyed by a moment of sorrow. This is how it worked. This is how it had always worked; a tangle of seemingly insignificant moments strung together like a complicated tapestry, a poem that didn't rhyme.

Maybe one day Hannah will finally grow up. Maybe one day one of these little people will grow curious and climb out of the hole in which she cast them. Maybe, if she's lucky, she'll get to meet one of them face-to-face one day and it'll give her the kind of amelioration that had eluded her for so long. That eludes her still.

But until that moment, she'll just sit there above them. Doing her best. It's all she can do. She is the only resident of this lonely city. She is the progenitor of all that she sees. She is the oldest human being to ever walk the planet Earth. She is everything, she is infinitely Hannah, the puppet with no strings, the Queen of the Dirt.

And she watches her creation dance.

DANGER SLATER is the world's most flammable writer. He is not the author of Moby Dick or Don Quixote, but he did write a few other (slightly less famous) books that you can currently check out, including Love Me, DangerRama and I Will Rot Without You, so that's pretty good too, right? RIGHT??? Originally from New Jersey, he now resides in Portland, OR.

For somewhat up-to-date information, please visit: danger-slater.blogspot.com

Lightning Source UK Ltd.
Milton Keynes UK
UKHW041534130619
344366UK00001B/37/P